The Last Tiger

Tony Black

Cargo Publishing

The Last Tiger

Tony Black

First Published in 2014

Published by Cargo Publishing

SC376700

Copyright © Tony Black 2014

ISBN 978-1-908885-55-5

Printed and bound by Bell and Bain, Glasgow

Typeset and designed by Cargo Publishing
www.cargopublishing.com

Also available as:
Kindle Ebook
EPUB Ebook

Unexpected, moving and magical. A new direction for Tony ,lack, and a bold one too."
Emlyn Rees, International bestseller

A rare and heartfelt fable of an immigrant boy torn between his ears for an endangered species and the father who's employed ） kill off what remains of that breed."
Paul Sayer, Whitbread-winning author

It's great, a real departure from the dark arts of crime fiction ）ut a successful one as it creates a genuinely engaging picture ）f strangers in a strange land, as well as carving a haunting space between historical reality and timeless fable."
~Nick Barlay, Granta 'Best of Young British Novelists'

"In this, his next book, Tony Black demonstrates what a talented and versatile writer he is. We're in Tasmania with a family of immigrants and the father is paid to hunt the very last Tasmanian tiger - and his son is horrified. His prose is at times spare and at times poetic as Tony delivers up a fascinating and moving novel about family ties and the truths we don't want to face."
~Michael Malone, author of The Guillotine Choice

"The Last Tiger is beautifully told - the nearest a novel could come to poetry without being such. The descriptions are rich and vivid, the reader is entirely immersed in the family's lives and their tribulations ... A powerful tale of man and the environment."
~Goodreads, five-star review

04994923

For my wife and son

Chapter One

In the distance, beyond Father's bowed head, below the river's swell and past the few great trees that once stood surrounded by forest, there were people, waiting.

"Why do they come, Mama?" I asked.

"They come to wait for the ship, Myko."

My mother raised her hand to shield her eyes and peered to the skies; the hot sun drew all the colour from the land. "They come and we will all meet them together, here, where we will make our new home."

Mother paused, then stooped before me. For a moment I caught sight of the tears in her eyes. I had seen so many of her tears on our voyage that I did not know what to say or do. I turned to see if my brother, younger than me by one year, had an answer, but it was just an instinct; at once I remembered he was gone from us.

Where I stood my mother held me tightly, but I did not struggle; I knew she wished to hide her tears from me. I rested my face upon her shoulder and watched the wide open country unfolding. I saw the snow-capped ridges of the mountains, small but rugged. Past the grassy plains and the river valleys I saw the dense woods and the impassable rainforests, and as we came closer to the island I saw the button grass plains and the distant mountain ranges. They were surrounded in forest and stretched as far as my gaze carried into this new land.

At first sight of the island my father bent over as if in prayer and laid his head upon the gunwale. "Van Diemen's Land," he sighed. "Van Diemen's Land, Van Diemen's Land," he said over and over quietly to himself.

A shiver passed through Father and he touched his heart, as if to check its beat. I had never before seen weakness in my father – even when he returned broken and wounded from battle, he held his head high. My mother's sobs shook me as I watched my father folded over before us, and my own heart began to pound loudly.

As the bosun approached, he laid the flat of his hand upon Father's back and spoke; "You know, that name has not been used for fifty years."

The sun cut creases in the bosun's face as he stood in its glare and chopped the air with his hand, motioning me to relay his words in the old language. I tried to do as he said but my father merely made a cross of his brows, straightened his broad back, and walked away to stand gazing into the clouds, alone.

I stepped from my mother's arms and the brief freedom felt like a gift to me as I approached the bosun. "What name does the island use?" I said.

The bosun opened wide his oil-black fingers and, with a sweep of his hand, pointed to the green land we approached. The tree trunks were etched white in the sun, against the pale blue of the sky. "Well," he said, "in the last century, the mighty British Empire sent ships full of convicts to this island."

I did not know the word he used. "What are convicts?" I asked; much of this new language was still strange to me.

"Thieves, mainly," said the bosun, "but rougher yet, all manner of lawbreakers and dogs." He jutted his hands together. "They came here held in chains, in the thousands they came, dumped on the island like England's refuse!"

The bosun slitted his eyes and trained them on me. "Upon this island, my boy, the wild sons of convicts roam …" He laughed and ruffled my straw-blond hair with his hand. "The island's fathers wanted to hide this past so they shed the fearsome name of Van Diemen's Land and now they call it, Tasmania."

"Tasmania," I said, testing the new word. The bosun tipped back his head and smiled as I spoke.

"Tasmania," I said again; the word sounded strange upon my tongue.

As the ship drew close to the island's shores I saw the green paddocks, with their dark wrinkles and rust-coloured tracks cut by the flocks and herds. The treetops reflected the sunlight which landed on the highest points, where sea birds soared in the skies above. I had never seen anything like the vast span of their wings as they glided across the island.

"Are there still convicts here?" I asked the bosun.

White smile lines cut into the corners of the bosun's eyes. "No, my boy," he said, "not in the year 1909 … but these are still wild lands, Tasmania has its tigers."

"Tigers!" The word jabbed a needle of ice in my belly. The thought of an encounter with a tiger – an animal I had only seen in picture books – made me wonder what would become of us all. Would we be attacked? Would we be killed? What other strange beasts roamed the island?

The bosun leaned down low before me, his forehead loomed over his round eyes like a high tombstone. "Yes, there are tigers," he said, dark tones leaping in his voice, "great fearsome beasts – fangs bigger than any shark's, they have!"

The bosun's tale came as steadily as the plink, plink, plink of raindrops; I felt my eyes widening and my mouth drooping with every new word. At once I wanted to be back in the Sakiai, where we were once happy, all together as a family.

The bosun crouched down low and sat on his heels; his belly protruded like a stuffed grain sack above his belt and he was close enough for me to smell the pipe tobacco on his breath. "Not a corner of this island is untouched by the tigers, my boy, they roam everywhere. See, it's their island, they know it's no place for a man. Hell, they've a right to it too."

"Why?" I asked, my voice weakening, twitches and tremors passing through me.

The bosun leaned forward; his shirtfolds filled with flesh and his shoulders became rounded. "I could tell you a hundred stories, maybe even a thousand, all reasons why those beasts and man were never meant to live side by side." He flicked his eyes to draw me closer and whispered, "Once I heard there was a tiger snatched a babe from its mother's arms – devoured it whole, before the poor woman's very eyes."

I pictured the bloody image and I shut tight my eyes to force it out, but it stayed, until I heard my mother calling me to her side: "Come here at once, Myko, come, we must prepare."

The bosun snatched off his hat and clutched it to his chest. His eyes widened above glowing cheeks as red as berries. Then he stared, fixed on me for a moment, and lunged forward with a playful snarl, "*Rarrr …*"

I flinched and jumped back from him and the bosun began to laugh loudly. He snarled again, like a tiger, and then waved me off, back to my mother.

The sun shone brightly and a strong breeze sprayed the deck and all upon it. The sea scent came sharply to my nostrils as my mother reached for my coat buttons, rummaging to fasten them. At twelve years of age I felt too old for her attentions. I wanted to push away her delicate fingers, but I could tell as she wrapped me up tightly that her thoughts were with my brother.

I thought of Jurgis too. At the start of our journey we dreamed of all the motor cars and tall buildings we would see. But as we neared port I knew now that this was not a place like the America we had set sail for.

I looked to my father, still crouched upon the gunwale. He held his head within his hands now, his fingers clutched so tightly it were as though he tried to stop the insides from bursting upon the spray wet boards at his feet. I stared at him for a moment

10

and suddenly, as though I willed it, his gaze fell upon me.

I pulled away from my mother at once. "Leave me be," I said. My words were harsh, and I quickly regretted how they sounded, but Mother sensed I meant her no harm and moved back.

I watched her step lightly away from me; as she went, she looked slight enough to be carried by the breeze to Father's side. She began to gently stroke my father's neck with her handkerchief, and then she removed the small piece of lace to dab at her wet eyes. She spoke softly to keep her words from me, but I was still close enough to hear; "How can we live in this place?" she said.

Father lowered his hands and looked up at my mother, his eyelids were white and heavy, as if they longed to be closed forever upon the world outside. "I have no idea," he said.

As I stood alone and watched my parents together I wanted to run to them, to know all would be well, but something held me where I was. I did not move as the passengers crowded on deck and the ship sailed nearer port. The sea breeze was crisp and fresh, alive with a strange tang carried from the approaching island. Soon more people surged around me, their fingers clutched at blanket rolls and tightly-packed market baskets.

"Myko, Myko …" Mother called out to me, "come here, we must stay together."

"What is that smell, Mama?"

"The smell?"

"Yes, out there." I pointed over the blue of the sea to the island.

My mother followed my fingertip and lifted her head to the breeze. "That is, I think, the eucalyptus trees, Myko. Do you like it?"

"No," I said. My reply was firm.

"But why, Myko? It is such a sweet smell."

I shook my head. "I don't like it."

I saw the faces in the crowd remove their hats and fly them in the air. Bodies were packed tightly around me, clammy hands touched my face as people pulled themselves forward, struggling to see the land come into view. I was scarcely able to move as a man appeared from high above us and called out, "*Hobart.*"

The deck applauded when the port was hailed, but neither my parents nor I joined in with the crowd's cheers.

Chapter Two

At dock the friendly bosun shook all our hands. Father reached out to him, I saw him place an item in the bosun's pocket but it was removed and returned quickly to him. I could not see what the item was, it was very small. My mother kissed the bosun upon the face; as she did so he smiled, and then he was gone from us, back to the decks of the ship which had carried us across the oceans, to what we did not know.

As we stood on the shore of our new land we watched the great hoists lower boxes of possessions onto the docks, but we had nothing.

People flowed like oats from a cut bag towards the township: broad men in oilskins and pale women clutching their bonnets in the heat of the shadeless day. Carts came to carry off grog barrels and the road was churned up with lazy wheel tracks as clouds of dry red dust rose all around.

I heard caged chooks squawk and I saw them worry at the pins that fastened them in, as everywhere, the sun-burnt faces of the Tasmanians stared on, mouths as wide to the air as fresh-landed cod.

"Myko, what is the matter?" said Mother; I saw the words itched at her. "Why are you so nervous?"

I shifted from side to side, all the while turning back to check what was behind me. My skin crawled in horror as the hot sun painted a yellow blanket over us. "It's nothing," I said. I tried to reassure my mother, "It's just all so new … that's all."

The men leaned against walls, the heels of their sturdy boots dug into the ground like dung forks. Some filled pipes from snout bags and some merely rested with thumbs in dusty waistcoats, hostile black eyes creeping beneath their hat brims.

Mother turned her attentions from me to brush at my

father's shoulders with her open hand. "Where has all this dust come from?" she said, as her hand made a drum beat on my father's broad back.

"It is the sun," said Father, his words slow and cautious, "it dries everything and when the people move about it goes up in the air." My father knelt down and took up some dry soil in his fingers; as we watched the grey soil drain from his fist, the small grains crumbled to dust and were carried away by the breeze.

Father stood up and wiped his hands together – I thought he might speak, but he said nothing, he merely squinted at the sun and sighed.

I watched Father's chest rise and fall as he stood before us, as straight as a milled log. His eyes darted quickly about and then fell into the shadows of his skull as the sun laced into his brows. As I watched him I saw the white cotton collars of his shirt were frayed at their edges.

"We must eat, we are all hungry," said Mother as she lifted her gaze and quickly ran her tongue over her pale lips.

Father looked about him, down towards the town, and once more to the ship we had just left. His mouth remained shut tight, like a thin wound, and then he dug in his pocket and looked at his timepiece. "We will have to find a store," he said. His eyes stayed on the pocket watch as he started to walk.

"It was your father's," said Mother. Little muscles began to twitch at the sides of her face as she spoke.

"We must eat," said Father.

Mother's words rippled like a stream, "But … but …"

"We must eat."

Father held tight to the pocket watch as he broke into his stride, and the hanging chain leaped at his side, cutting through the sun's beams, catching the rays and glistening like the sea beyond. Mother and I followed behind as Father guided the

14

way; his steps were long and full of purpose and I had to move quickly to keep pace with him.

Sand-coloured buildings shimmered around us as we passed through town, the yellow stones looked as if they would wash away with the rain. I reached out to touch them – they were warm in the sun, but they were course and rough-hewn, and nothing like the buildings I had known.

"This will do," said Father as he stopped outside a shop.

I looked up towards the shop's sign. "What is it?" I asked.

No one answered me. My mother and father stood staring at each other for a long time and then I spoke again. "What is this place?"

Father turned to face me. "It is a pawnbroker's shop, Myko."

The shop's sign fluttered as the shore breeze whistled around the door jamb and a bell clanged as we entered.

Inside a corridor ran to the back porch where I saw the pawnbroker resting in a rope hammock. "Just a minute," he called out. His words were followed by loud rasping coughs. As he stood up the pawnbroker put his hands to his back and pressed in his lumbar like he was easing into a tight girdle. "Just coming … I'm just coming now, won't be more than a few moments."

As I looked up and down the store shelves I saw there was a row of stout jugs and little kegs behind the counter. Canned goods and flannel shirts were piled high on a table, while heavy horse blankets were stored underneath. Tin cups and frying pans hung on pot hooks everywhere and fancy goods, silver buttons and knife blades, shone from behind glass-fronted showcases.

"Good day," called out the pawnbroker as he came through to the store's front. His skin was dark and shiny from the sun's hammering; deep furrows were cut above his nose and around his eyes. "Now … how can I be of assistance?"

My father held out his pocket watch and I saw that, even indoors, it shone brightly. There were no markings on the timepiece but I could see the fine movements inside when the pawnbroker raised it to his eye. He did not seem to be interested and I felt glad; I did not want my father to sell his pocket watch.

"Hmnn," said the pawnbroker. As he turned down the corners of his mouth two rows of dark crescents appeared on either side of his face. His skin was crossed with lines and darkly freckled and I did not like to look at him.

I turned away to paw at bolts of cloth and square-toed boots, when suddenly my gaze was yanked to the wall behind the counter. An animal skin was hung proud of the store's goods; it was not very large, about the size of a farm dog.

As I gulped my breath, I counted thirteen dark black stripes down the back of the olive-brown skin. There had been cuts made, the ears and paws were removed and I thought it was an unfortunate beast; its thirteen stripes had proved unlucky indeed.

I wanted to take down the animal skin, to stroke the pelt and feel what was once a real creature. What was it? Where did it come from?

The pawnbroker caught me looking and put down Father's pocket watch. "Like it, boy?"

I did not speak. I still could not look at the little man.

"Shot it myself," he said, swiping away a blowfly with the back of his bony hand. "Do you know what it is?"

As I turned to face the pawnbroker my jaw clenched and there was a dry copper taste in my mouth as I wondered if I would fly at him with my fists. Why did he kill this beast? What harm had it done him?

"Myko," said Mother. Her eyes prompted me to remember my manners – I did not want to see Mother frown on me – I

16

turned to face the pawnbroker squarely and shook my head.

"Tiger!" he said. His face brightened; two full rosebuds flowered on his cheeks. "It's a bounty kill, that's why the ears and paws are cut off, so it can't be claimed on twice."

I felt as if a coil of hot iron twisted through me. It touched my heart first and then settled in my belly, where it turned and turned again. How could such an animal, which had once roamed free, be cut down like this? Why would any man want to kill it?

"Yes, that's a Thylacine, the Tasmanian tiger all right," said the pawnbroker, smiling to himself.

My heart beat faster; as I moved closer to the tiger skin the bosun's words were in my ears again. I had seen my first Tasmanian tiger, but it seemed nothing like the fearsome creature he'd described.

As my eyes burned on the tiger I willed it to live again. I knew this tiger was gone forever – but I wanted to see it come alive, to right the wrong which had been done it. I hoped the bosun's words were true – that this island was the tigers' – that I would soon see them wherever they roamed.

I turned to see the pawnbroker remove his eyeglass. He counted out loud, touching the fingers of his left hand with his right forefinger, and then he announced loudly, "Five. I'll pay five pounds for the timepiece."

Father did not seem to understand; he shook his head at me.

"Five," said the pawnbroker again, raising up five fingers to show what his offer was. As he began to count out the money to my father, I saw dark brown freckles moving on the pawnbroker's hairless head. It was a small head, narrow and flat, and I wondered did it ever hold any thoughts other than the counting of money.

When he finished dropping the last of the slow trickle of

coins into Father's hand the pawnbroker looked suddenly into Father's eyes. "Have you just arrived?" he said.

Father turned to me, as I had learned our new language faster than my parents, and I pointed back to the ship. "Yes," I said. My voice was strong now, I felt I had the measure of the pawnbroker. "We are from the ship."

He leaned forward and rested his elbow on the counter. "Well, have you people any place to stay?"

His words were the same as the bosun's, but he formed them in a different way and I had to listen very carefully to understand.

I turned to my father. "He wants to know where we will be staying, since we have come to the island?"

Father shrugged his heavy shoulders and we turned back to the pawnbroker.

"Well, that's just grand," the pawnbroker said, parting the air with his hand, "just grand indeed."

Father and Mother smiled at each other. I could see they thought the pawnbroker was about to welcome them to the island as a friend, as they would have done for strangers in their own home. But their smiles did not stay on their faces for long.

The pawnbroker snatched back the coins from Father's hand and quickly dropped them inside his chamois pouch, fastening it tightly with a flourish of his wrist. "Yes sir, that's just grand … I'm in a position to assist you good folks to find your way quickly, being as I am what you might call well connected hereabouts."

The pawnbroker quickly leaned over the counter and grasped my father's hand tightly. My father looked confused; his eyes widened as his arm was fiercely shaken up and down. Only the pawnbroker seemed pleased as he grinned widely, showing teeth like black-rotten fence staves, before dancing off to swipe again at blowflies with his ledger.

Chapter Three

We wended our way north, on the cart of a merchant haulier from Hobart. The bushcutters were still at work, clearing the way for the packhorse.

"These roads are no better than tracks," said Father, staring into the wind as it blew through the weed-wreathed rocks.

The dry baked clay was hard-packed beneath the cartwheels and crackled as we went. "Be careful, Myko," said Mother, as she reached above me to snatch at the dipping branches that were scratching at our heads, poking and prodding to keep us from rest.

The sky's bone-white clouds, which followed us from the township, turned grey as stone as rain picked up. It was heavy rain, unlike any we had ever known, and I grew wet-through quickly. Lorikeets and orange-bellied parrots sheltered on the branches above us and cried out as we approached, flapping their wings in defiance.

"Myko, come here to me," said Mother. She tried to draw me closer to her side in the back of the cart but I stayed by the edge.

"No, Mama," I said, as I eyed the dark recesses of the forest, wondering what lurked within.

"Myko, come here …" Mother held out her arms to me, and she motioned me to huddle at her side.

I shook my head. I would not move and soon my mother lowered her reach from me. I saw brownish glints shining near her eyes as her long black hair sat flat upon her brow and around her face like a cowl.

"Father, where are we going?" I asked.

"To Woolnorth," he said; his voice was flat and hollow.

"What is Woolnorth?" I asked.

My father shifted to face me. He raised his hat and shook out the rain before replacing it upon his head. "The Van Diemen's Company sheep station is at Woolnorth." His eyes looked dully before him. "I hope to find work there."

My father pulled his hat's brim over his face and he folded his arms across his chest, letting out a sigh. I knew there would be no more questions answered by him this day.

I watched the sky above turn the colour of an old skillet's base. The rain continued to pound as constantly as a mill-wheel turns and the cold of the coming night's chill settled all around us. I longed to be indoors and warm, by our homefire in the Sakiai perhaps, but we were far from such comforts now.

The rugged crags of the rock face towards the far blue hills soon came upon us. Rumpled grey paddocks drew nourishment from the hills' lee and the weak sun placed a yellow lantern's glow on the rain-washed summit.

The wet trees cut out along the horizon turned black against the purple sky. The trees' roots, sparkling like silver buckles, looked as if they might run towards us and sweep us up above the waist-deep wattle, to I knew not where.

The haulier grunted and drew the cart to a halt. The packhorse stumbled, his legs continuing to rise up and down where he stood. "Whoa," called out the haulier, lashing the packhorse's back with a heavy stock whip.

The animal whinnied and was still; as the haulier turned, dark shadows drew the silhouette of his timber-black features on the canvas packs. "This is as far as I go," he said.

Father tipped back his hat and a river of rain flowed from its brim and down his back. For a moment my father had no words, he merely scanned the pouring skies and the dark forest, but then he spoke.

"This is Woolnorth?" His voice carried disbelief.

The haulier coughed and spat a heavy gobbet of phlegm

from his mouth. He leaned back towards us in the cart's rear, then twisted long-necked to point out a muddy trail. "Up that track," he said.

Dense black branches hung low above the dark trail. I felt the night's breeze upon my cheek and my heart's glass shell trembled. The smell of the cart's sour oldness had grown to feel like a comfort to me.

"This is as far as I go," said the haulier, his voice rising above the pound of the rain. "Out … out!"

The packhorse seized the load and tried to make off once more as the haulier shouted, "Whoa, whoa," and brought the stock whip down again, "stupid animal … now *out* the lot of you, this is as far as I go!"

My mother turned to look at Father. "Petras … this cannot be right."

The cart swayed from side to side as my father stood up and moved towards the haulier. "Here?" he said, "are you sure?"

Father arched his back, leaning over the cart rails to face the haulier. He held open his hands as he spoke, his shoulders bunched tight under his wet coatfolds. "This is Woolnorth … this is where we will find the sheep station?"

The haulier puffed his cheeks as Father spoke. He looked ready to release a gale of wind from the tight slit of his mouth. "Out. Out. Out," he roared, knocking away Father's hands with the handle of his stock whip.

As we stepped down from the cart, we were forced to walk bent to the wind, deep in the wet mud of the track. Like a family of rats we were drenched black by the rain.

"Stay close, Myko," said Mother. As she shuddered beneath her dark shawl each new gust of wind made her flinch and shiver and take a wheeze of indrawn breath.

"We cannot walk far like this." Mother held up one of our chaff bags, which carried all our possessions. "Do you hear me,

Petras? We cannot walk far like this … the wind could raise him from his boots."

Father turned to me and looked down where I stood.

"Come, Myko …" he said, "climb on my back."

My father sat down on his haunches and patted his shoulder, twice. His eyes were wide and white in the dark of the night.

"No. I will walk by myself," I said.

"Myko!" said Mother.

"I will walk. I will walk," I shouted to them, as I brushed past my father.

The track soon opened up and gave way onto flooded paddocks. The pasture land was hidden beneath trembling grey sheets that stretched as far as we could see.

Father shook his head; "I hope they have gathered the flocks," he said. "Come, we will try the shearers' cottages."

At the first door Father knocked upon we were confronted by an unfriendly Irishman.

The Irishman's eyes were vicious; a mix of red and yellow ringed the rusty pennies of their centres. As he squared his shoulders and walked out of his shearer's cottage, his barrel chest pointed at us.

"Go back where ye came," he said. When the Irishman spoke he pressed his tongue upon his teeth forcing out a clacking noise that was followed with a heavy breath of spittle.

Father stood his ground before the Irishman and we sunk behind his greatcoat like field mice avoiding the sweep of a plough.

"I said, go back," said the Irishman. "Go, go away with ye!"

My father kept still and did not alter his stance. The Irishman had many years on Father; as he stepped forward I could see the grey wending its way through his hair like the ocean's waves.

No words passed between the two men. I believed I heard the sound of the Irishman's breath as my mother reached out her thin arm to tug at my father's coattail.

The air was thick with threats and I was sure there would be conflict.

Soon the Irishman leaped into a jaunty stride and began to walk a circle around my father. I watched intently, I dared not move my eyes for one moment. The two men were like fighting dogs sizing each other before their attack – but neither man was willing to make the first lunge.

Only Father's eyes moved with the Irishman's steps. He watched him carefully, like a hunting bird watches its prey before sweeping and claiming its kill. I saw my father's neck was tensed; long lines of muscle and sinew stood out like steel rods. He was ready to deflect blows – but they did not come – the Irishman merely hacked up a mouthful of spit and threw it on the ground.

As the Irishman eyed my calm father, his stare subsided; his temper was no more a threat than a damp powder flask. Suddenly, with great flurry, he threw up his hands and stamped indoors.

Behind us a voice called out above the wind and rain, "Fair play to you, sir! Fair play indeed!"

Beside a barn some men gathered, huddled at the gable end like worshippers beneath a church apse. The men wore shirtsleeves folded past the elbow, their thumbs tucked within dark waistcoats. Some wore stovepipe hats tipped far back upon their heads and they all stood firm in great heavy, thick-soled bluchers laced above the ankle.

"Best leave the old Irish alone," called a man at the front. He was small with narrow shoulders; a neat scarf was tied around his neck like a bandage that was there to protect his throat. "He thinks he owns the station, been here man and boy."

My father looked down at me in his usual way but I was too slow to convey the man's words.

"Come in out of the cold, we have a grand fire roaring in the barn," he called out again.

We followed the crowd inside. There were children playing on the hay bales and women boiling billycans by the fire. We were a great spectacle for all of a few minutes and then the curiosity subsided and we were just another one of the many dirt poor families who made the journey northwards, to seek work upon the land.

Chapter Four

The man who called us into the billet was known as Nathaniel.

"You must be hungry," he said. He took a little wrap of flour from his swag and poured it in a pan. "I'll cook up some Johnnycakes for you to eat by the fire … will make you feel quite at home."

Mother tugged at my wet coat and in her hands she rung my heavy wet sleeves, which left a grey pool on the dusty floor. "Come, Myko … sit by the fire where it is warm, you must dry yourself."

I did as I was told and sat upon the flat, warm hearthstone next to Nathaniel. A barefoot girl in long trousers came to sit opposite me, pulling in her legs and resting her chin on her knees before smiling broadly at me.

Where I sat the smell from the cooking rose in time with the steam from my wet clothes.

"So, why have you come to Woolnorth?" asked Nathaniel.

My father was slow to answer, his eyes dimmed and his few words thinned to none. I knew he thought little of the place we had set the last of our hopes upon.

"Well," said Nathaniel, "I come from free-settler roots. My family farmed an isle in Scotland, ran sheep there for all their lives. But the owner cleared them to make way for more sheep and bigger profits!"

"How did you come to be here?" said Mother, "it is such a long way from your homeland."

Nathaniel stepped back from the fireside. "Well, my forebears were packed off to the New World, weren't they? So here I am," he waved a long wooden fork as he spoke. The smell of the Johnnycakes made me hungry.

"I know nothing of my heritage, save a song or two my

mother sang me as a child." The screech of Nathaniel's voice seemed to be at home in Tasmania, as much as the natter of crickets that filled the night air around us.

"I myself crossed the Tasman Strait to seek my fortune in a gold rush … but my claim was slow on paying, so here I now am!"

Father stood to face Nathaniel squarely. "There is work here?"

"Well, sir," said Nathaniel, who was clear-eyed, his words coming easily to his tongue, "there is no shortage of work hereabouts. I've seen this billet packed tighter than this, I think the elements have seen many off. Do you know this work?"

Father said nothing in reply and Nathaniel's eyes dug deep holes in him. "Do you know the beasts we run here, sir?"

My father's brows levelled on his face for the first time in the listless night; "I am a shepherd," he said.

Nathaniel returned to the fire and scooped up the Johnnycakes, they sizzled as he flopped them out of the pan and onto the plate. "All well and good, sir, all well and good."

I grabbed my plate and devoured the food, as keenly as I did Nathaniel's words.

"But let me tell you this, sir … I'll wager none of your shepherding has prepared you for life on Van Diemen's. No sir. We have flocks, that is true, among the mightiest yet seen, flocks by the thousand … but we have more besides."

Nathaniel stood in front of the fire warming his thin legs in its glow; the dim light threw an orange band around his high-domed head. "Yes, we have more besides indeed."

Father sat back and rested deeper in his chair; a brassy glare filled his eye as he finished chewing his small bite of food. "I have heard of your tigers," he said bluntly.

The word sent prickles up my spine; as I looked at my father I felt his hot stare lower a web of shame over me.

"Your tigers do not frighten me," said Father.

"Oh, you have heard of the tigers … have you, now?" said Nathaniel. He shook his head with doubt; it was as if he alone could question another on such a thing. He walked from the smoke-blackened hearthstone with his eyes raised all the way up to the roof's arch.

"We have many wolves in my own country, I know how they are," said Father. Nathaniel laughed. "Wolves … give me a pack of snarling, blood hungry wolves over a solitary one of Tasmania's tigers on any day!" He shook his head once more and returned to face the fire. As he took a pouch of tobacco from his waistcoat he began to fill a long clay pipe. Nathaniel lit the pipe with a taper and the charred and aromatic smell of smoking tobacco leaped all around us. Dismissively, Nathaniel turned to my father. "What have you heard of the tiger?"

Father's face was stern; as he opened his large hands their shadows played like marionettes upon the floor's boards. "It is but a dog, a hyena with stripes," he said.

Nathaniel laughed loudly, and suddenly more laughter echoed around the room as a group rose like an angry sea at Nathaniel's side. He kept back the gathering with his outstretched palms, and then he held his breath before us for a moment and the room fell silent.

I could hear the night's rhythm drumming beyond the window's pane. Slow grey swirls rose from Nathaniel's pipe and curled towards the roof's dip. I could see the skin on Nathaniel's face stretched tight by the sun. The tip of his nose set in a hook. "Let me ask you," he said, as he pointed the end of his pipe at Father, "what dog, or even wolf for that matter, have you seen separate a mob of sheep in fifty different directions by merely being within a mile?"

Nathaniel leaned back and placed the pipe between his teeth; it clacked like throwing dice. "Or, for that matter," he lunged forward, jutting out his jaw, "what dog or wolf, have you seen send a packhorse, a group of oxen, or any hunting dogs whimpering with fear? My own beasts have cowered at my back like little children at one whiff of a tiger. I have seen game in the bush run terrified, panting, their hearts ready to burst inside them, a full hour before any tiger has shown itself!

There was a fierce glint in Nathaniel's eye and when I saw it I wanted to throw up my heels and run, but I could not.

I felt the rim of my panic rising as the room suddenly fell silent once more, and then a tall man with a white face stepped forward.

"They are no ordinary animal," he said. His head was clear of any hair, but long dark wisps hung like branches below his ears and upon his face. "They are our terror."

Father reclined his head and folded his arms across his belly. He seemed disbelieving, but his face said he would not mock at these fears.

Within the billet, as I watched Nathaniel and the crowd stooped before us, my thoughts ran as hot as a pyre. When the settlers spoke their stories gave me the same feeling I had in the Sakiai, listening to tales of *Giltine* – the bringer of death.

The current of the night's talk carried us to a dark place. As the tall man stepped forward he brought a rush of air towards us. His waxy skin hid heavy tracks, as wide as grill markings, on the sides of his face.

"They do not hunt or kill like other animals," he said softly, and the stiffness of his voice betrayed a threat of tears. "They attach to the throat of their prey, then they drink out their blood … like vampires."

"They eat nothing else," burst out Nathaniel, "nothing! They merely drink their blood … What kind of a fiend lives that way?"

I stood by Mother and Father at the fireside. I looked in

their eyes but I saw no hint of their thoughts. My mother's mouth was open like a coin pouch.

"They eat nothing else?" said Father.

"Sometimes, they will eat the heart," said Nathaniel. "I have watched them. They are not afraid of us, they act as if we are not there. Once I emptied a pistol shot into the withers of a large male – he was going for my sheep hound, Bess. She were afraid of him and ran like the blazes at first, but then took charge of herself when I closed them in the pen. I could only get one shot off for fear of hitting Bess; there was an almighty tussle in that sheep pen but the bullet never slowed the tiger one bit. I could only watch as he put those grand jaws of his around poor Bess's skull. My, what a gape it were, I swear he could have swallowed whole my best bull's head. She fell dead that second, the beast had crushed her skull in its jaws.

"I ran to get my Winchester, I was going to plug him good and raw, but then he took the side of the pen in one great leap, like a kangaroo, it were, I swear. That pen was six feet high, and he jumped it like I cross a stile. Now none of this is bullyragging, that I assure to you. I watched that beast like you watch me now. I was glad to see him running, I still say today the next bullet from that handgun would have been best fired in my own head. I do believe the tiger could have taken the full round before he fell down and I was not the man to try it."

I listened to the tales until my mother approached me. She placed her hands upon me, patting my clothes. "Good, you are dry. I think you should take your bunk now."

"But, Mama …"

"No, Myko, it is time for you to rest now. Go to your bunk."

As I lay awake my thoughts were a hot broth, bubbling inside of me. I saw again the mangy pelt which hung in the pawnbroker's shop, the bounty on it already claimed. I knew now that every hand on the island was turned against the tiger.

"You do not like it here, do you?" said a soft voice at my side. I turned but I saw no one beyond the darkness.

"Who is that?" I said.

Someone struck a match and lit a candle, and across the bunk room I saw the barefoot girl. "I am Tilly," she said.

As she walked over to face me I saw pale bluebells covered her flannel nightgown. Her small feet poked beneath, as freckled as her wide face.

"Oh, it's you," I said and looked away.

The girl sat down on the empty bunk beside me, "What is wrong?"

"Nothing is wrong … go away!"

"I can tell you do not like it here."

I spoke flatly: "No. I do not like it here."

"Do you miss your home?"

I turned over in the bunk and showed the girl my back.

"Are you frightened? Is it the talk of tigers?"

"No!" I snapped. I sat upright in the bunk. "I just don't like how they talk about the tiger."

The girl curled up her nose. "They hate the tigers."

Her words lit a flame in me; I jumped from the bunk to stand before her. "Why? What has the tiger done that is so bad?"

She dropped her eyes and began to play with the sleeve of her nightgown. "I don't know … they just hate it," she said, "and that's why they kill them, and tell tales at night around the fireside."

I turned away and slumped back in my bunk, and the girl looked at me. "That's just how it is here," she said, "that's how it's always been."

Chapter Five

In the months before our voyage from the Sakiai in Lithuania my brother Jurgis and I waited for the stork with the rest of the village. Father placed a cartwheel high upon our rooftop, hoping the stork would land on our home and build its nest. "If the stork rests here it will bring us luck and fortune," he said, "would that not be good, my boys?"

The air was cold and still, but Father worked bare-chest as he hoisted high the wooden cartwheel and tied it into place on our rooftop. "This is a special day, my boys," he said, "the stork is the holiest of birds … we must make our roof look the most tempting to land upon in the whole village."

As Father gritted his teeth, he forced the cold air from his nostrils and tied tight the jute rope to secure the cartwheel. Whilst he worked, his nails dug into the wet blackness of the wood that held our roof. "There, it is good enough for any stork," he said. When he was finished he stood smiling and placed his foot on the cartwheel's rim. "Not one would pass it by. We will have fine fortunes this year, my boys, mark my words, we will have the stork land right here and we will be blessed!"

There was great excitement awaiting the stork's arrival. Mother tended the homefire and baked bread called *duona*. Some of the women from the village brought gifts of fruits, chocolates or pencils and they hung coloured eggs on the tree branches.

"The stork must be coming soon," said one of the women, "look, those eggs are the stork's … they are, they are, can't you tell?"

Jurgis smiled and laughed out loud at the goings and some of the younger children began to lift their legs high in the air to walk with the gait of the stork. "They are sure there is luck coming," said Jurgis, "the stork's luck."

I was not so sure. "But how can the stork bring luck?" I said.

My brother looked at me but said nothing; he was too taken up with the excitement that was everywhere.

"Jurgis, I don't like this stork business," I said.

My brother's smile slipped away. "But why?"

"What if the stork is not caught? What then?"

As we looked to the sky, we saw no stork. For a long time we searched over every inch of the blue sky we could see, from the green pastures and the hilltops we searched ever upwards, but the stork did not come. And in time, everything was changed; the talk turned quickly to *Giltine* – the bringer of death.

"Without the stork, *Giltine* will surely walk among us," an old farmer said.

Another spoke of his flocks: "Without the presence of the stork, there will be losses, for *Giltine* makes all beasts uneasy; they take on strange unnatural behaviours and in flocks they scatter," he said.

I looked at my brother, and I saw that he stared at our father with wide eyes. "What is happening, Myko?" he said.

"I do not know." I was as confused as he was.

Our mother ran to us and held us to her, but she brought no comfort to us either; we heard only her sobs above the crowd's chatterings.

"I should have seen the signs," said a broad woman, a crone with night black hair, "I baked bread that broke clean into two parts in my oven, surely it was one of *Giltine's* messages."

"I had a crack appear in my ceiling," said another, "likewise, it fell into two parts … was this not one of *Giltine's* auguries?"

A loud whisper spread among the crowd and then

the beekeeper stepped forward. Everyone fell silent, as the beekeeper began to speak. "I found a cross-shaped honeycomb in one of my hives," he said.

Suddenly there was a noise like a giant gathering his breath. "But that is not all." The crowd fell silent once more as the beekeeper took up the story. "I then returned home to find my deerhound, an animal I loved as one of my own family, had devoured her entire litter of pups."

"It is *Giltine*," the people cried out, *"Giltine* is among us."

The villagers wailed and howled, men and women cried openly, and mothers clutched small children tight to their breasts as people fled in all directions.

In the days to come *Giltine* appeared again and again, in many new guises.

Chapter Six

The days passed at the great sheep station of Woolnorth with little flurry, save the harshness of the storm which descended upon us like a tidal wave.

It was a cruel time to be out of doors, even when the storm was spent. Grey skies, nearing on black, spread over the sedgeland covering the hills. The great white flocks scattered and huddled under leatherwoods, by lowland heaths, and along the hillsides' rocky bournes. Their shrill bleats were heard skirling all along the edge of the meadows.

The pasture's tree trunks wore a black-wet belt where the floodplains subsided, and the hopeless spray of raindrops from the ferns rose like mists upon the heavy air of the pulsing gales.

As I walked with my father in the morning's air he collected small dark-knotted branches from the ground. "Have you greased those boots, Myko?" he said.

"Yes."

"Like I showed you?"

"Yes, just like you showed me; look." I halted where I stood to show my boots; they shone like pearls.

"Good," said Father, "you have learnt that lesson well."

I followed him through the pasture land and, though I measured my steps with care, nothing kept the punishing wetness from my feet. The unpredictable wind lifted up stray flaps of clothing and crawled upon my skin like icy mites. I shivered uncontrollably.

"I will show you how to set snares," said Father, "you must use a strong stick on a straight treadle – like so." He raised a small branch before his eye and tested its suppleness in his hands.

"You see, the grasp must be light." My father was close

enough for me to note the flecks of red inside his eyes. "Do you understand?"

I nodded to him, "Yes, I see."

Father took great care with his instructions. He looked at me with caution, searching to be sure I had grasped his meaning.

"I understand, Father," I said as I scowled at the sky, waiting for the sun's warmth to show. I flapped my arms and patted at the sleeves of my heavy-flannel overshirt.

"Good, then set the snares there," said Father, as he stopped his instructions and took himself to rest upon a five-bar gate. He pointed me down the track, which made a thin dog-leg towards the blur of green which marked the forest. As I set about tying the snares, he watched closely, squinting beneath the brim of his hat for some minutes, before he made to leave. "They are good," he shouted to me over his shoulder as he went, "now go along the fence, tie more, and remember what I have taught you."

I saw men fencing around the paddocks. As I went, they hammered heavy palings and twisted great reels of wire between them. There seemed to be many men at this task, stretching like a line of ants from the low foothills to the rocky rise beyond the paddocks.

The wind made my eyes tear-blown as I entered Spink's Paddock to set the necker snares, as Father had shown me. The sun was warming and a yellow sheet descended on the paddock. I crouched low among the smells of damp grass and the sounds of the rippling stream, which was darkly stained by the mud-flows, and then I heard my name searing the air.

"Myko. Myko. Myko."

I raised myself and turned to face the open paddock. I saw nothing, but heard the cry go up again.

"Myko ..."

This time, as I searched with my eyes, I found the

35

source of the noise. The voice came from the track, which led from the billet. Running hard on the wet trail was Tilly. She was barefoot and I could see the mud splashes following her steps.

"I am here," I called.

Tilly ran to me and as she neared I saw her long trousers, rolled past her knees, were soaked through.

"Myko ... Myko, you must come, quick," she said.

"Why?"

"You must! Come now."

She grabbed at my arm and tried to draw me into her stride. "Quick, Myko."

"But, why? What is it?"

"A hunt, there's a hunt."

I threw down the branches – the snares could wait.

As we ran, I tried to draw out some of Tilly's panic. "What are they hunting ... a tiger?"

Tilly's breath was heavy, but her words came clearly. "A pack of stray dogs has been seen on the station."

I had not seen any pack. "Dogs. From where?"

"They chased rabbits down from the gullies and now they're in the myrtle forest ... there are some on the company's lands, threatening the flocks."

We ran quickly, my heart was pounding, and then suddenly we were stopped still as the air rang through with rifle shots.

I turned to Tilly. "They're shooting."

"Yes. They're nearby."

A pocket of powder rose from the roof of a copse of trees.

"There, look." As I called out a large setter dog came loping from the bush into the open paddock, spreading the flocks where it ran. It shone red and bright as a newborn calf.

The setter's long and loping strides drew fast upon the

flock. I could tell the dog had just discovered a new and strange game; it had no hope of bringing down its quarry.

Another rifle shot rang out from the copse and the setter was dropped. Cheers filled the air as a group of men watched the dog writhing on the wet grass. I watched as it took its last few breaths, and then lay stilled.

The men lifted their hats above their heads and grinned wildly as they descended upon the paddock to retrieve their carcass.

Tilly and I ran towards the loud cheering crowd, where great excitement spread among the men. I watched them peer above the paddocks looking for more dogs, but they had been scattered.

We pressed our way to the crowd's front where the setter lay. The white prongs of the dog's ribcage showed above the dark red of its coat and the darker red of the bullet wound. It was a young dog, its eyes were black and shining in its peaceful face. It was not yet fully grown – its short coat lacked the coarseness of most pack dogs.

Where I stood, staring, I felt Tilly fidget at my side. She crouched low on the ground, beside the setter, and stroked the softness of its crown.

"Look," said Tilly, she eased open the setter's mouth.

I gazed at the dog's teeth and saw they were milk white and clean; they had never tasted mutton.

"Well, there he is," said the gunman; his eyes were wide-set and little lines cross-hatched their edges. "Was a strong looking beast."

The gunman saw us staring at the setter's teeth and tried to draw me to his sport. "I reckon he could have snatched out a sheep's throat with one bite of them teeth, what do you say, boy?"

I looked up to him, he was smiling. His dark sun-punished

skin was stretched taut to his face, his rifle butt perched upon his hip, like a figure from the cover of a penny novella.

"It's a bitch," I said, "she is very young."

The gunman's complexion quickly changed. His face turned hard and twisted as a walnut and then he showed his anger. I was pushed aside as he grabbed the setter by its scruff.

He held up the carcass and looked beneath its belly. "Of course it's a bitch … them's the hunters," he said.

The rest of the men laughed in little muffled bursts.

There were slaps placed upon the gunman's back and then the fencers moved off to return to their duties.

As they went, the gunman swung the setter above his shoulder like a hay bale, then threw it upon the dirt track which skirted the paddock.

"Damn dog," he said, spitting where it lay, as he made to join the others.

I felt an emptiness inside as I looked down upon the setter. Its eyes were bloodied and ruptured, its tongue swelled as wide as a water pouch within its mouth. I knew the Tasmanian devils would set upon the dog to feed. By the next day there would be scarce a bone left to see of the young animal.

"Boy, get back to them snares," called the gunman at me, his voice thumping like a piston, "that bitch'll be just one of many!"

The gunman turned from me and as I saw the back of his flat shoulders I felt the muscles of my jaw tighten. My head buzzed like insects over a billabong. I reached down to the ground and took up a heavy rock. I set my aim on his head, and drew back my arm.

"Myko!" called Tilly, "no …" She darted in front of me, wrestling the rock from my grasp and rolling it onto the ground below. I fought with Tilly to reach for the rock, but she held me back, her quick fingers covering my eyes. "Myko, you can't."

"Why not?" I stepped away from her; the braces that had sat on her shoulders hung behind her like coattails.

Tilly's eyes were wide as she looked at me. "Myko, it is just a dog."

I could not face her anymore, and turned away.

"Myko … Myko," she said as I moved off to be alone, "where are you going?"

I said nothing, as I ran quickly.

Chapter Seven

As soon as I arrived at the billet, I took the back of the station's grey mare. She was straight-backed and strong, at least sixteen hands high, and jumped the woodheap like she was taking flight.

I heard the rolling sea as I took the track to the headland gorse. It felt good to be putting distance between myself and the station as I pressed my feet in the stirrups and thundered through the boggy speargrass flats.

The sun came out and pressed itself on the sky like a medal, turning the air humid and syrupy as the wet land began to steam all around. I raced over the man ferns, which shook out their stores of raindrops, and I was soon on the track to the coastal grasslands.

The raw yellow of the beach was visible far below. Gannets and albatrosses fished out beyond the cliff edge in the darkness of the deep and green sea. The island looked calm now the sun had shown, and then the stillness was suddenly disturbed.

The grey stiffened her shanks and would not proceed. "Hup, hup," I yelled, "hup … go, go." I dug in my heels but it made no impact upon her. I slapped at her hinds, I dug harder at her sides, but she remained unmoving.

"What is it?" I said, "Why have you stopped?" The grey laid back her ears and refused to go forward. As she did so, two terriers which trailed us from the station crouched under her belly and bared their teeth.

"What's going on?" I said. I had never seen anything like this happen before, I had never known animals to show such fright.

As I climbed down and made to tie up the grey, I saw that her flanks were wet with mud and sweat, then suddenly she reared up like a circus horse.

"Whoa, whoa, girl," I said. I stepped before her and gently stroked her nose with my fingertips. "Whoa, whoa, girl," I said again.

I felt relieved to see the grey soon settled; I hitched her to a heavy sand-scoured piece of driftwood and proceeded upon the track by foot.

The sun shone high in the sky and the light dappled through the high branches which spread in a vault above the track. All around was the fresh smell of salt sprayed from the sea.

I heard gannets squawking and looked out to the ocean, where the white tide ate at the beach, when suddenly the strongest of scents dragged me back upon the track. The air was heavy with the smell. I saw nothing, but I knew it must be the animal scent that the grey and the terriers had sensed.

The track was empty, but then I heard a noise, a low muted tone like the cries of a baby.

What could it be? I wondered, no one leaves an infant alone on the coast.

I continued on the path and the crying grew clearer, though no louder. It was a painful cry, a plea for help. I knew that I was needed nearby and I felt my heart beating high in my chest, pressing on my throat.

I imagined what miseries must have befallen the poor creature making such frightened noises, but I found nothing, I saw nothing. Though the scent was at its strongest, I found not a trace of any living soul.

As I passed the path's wide curve I started to pray, I begged to be of use to the maker of these sounds. But my prayers were not answered and I drew in my fists and began to hold them tight, swinging out in quick sharp bursts of frustration.

As I lashed out, suddenly, the cries stopped. From the trackside, beneath a patch of bracken, burst a tiger. The yellow-brown of his coat flashed before my eyes. In one wild leap the tiger freed itself from a necker snare. He seemed to jump straight up into the air, above the full height of a man.

I watched, mesmerised; I had never seen a living tiger. He was a beautiful beast, a large bull tiger, at least seven feet from nose to tail.

As I watched him straighten his backbone I saw the black bands upon his rump; the stripes reached halfway along his body.

Here was the tiger I heard so much of. As he faced me now I sensed his strength. He stood in the track and set his eyes upon me. I felt my breath quicken and then slow into the lightest of gasps. I trembled with fear.

The thin sea breeze fed my thoughts. Should I run? I wondered, then, to where? I could not outrun a tiger. I could only stand before the tiger, knowing I was trapped.

As the heavy air carried the tiger's scent to me, I knew this was the beast which raided flocks and terrified settlers at its every turn. The beast of myth which stalked the island.

I had heard many stories of the tiger's ferocity. It crushed the skull of Nathaniel's sheephound with one bite of its mighty gape. I knew they said the tiger was no ordinary animal, I remembered the settlers told me: "It feasted only on the blood of its victims, and sometimes, the heart."

My pulse throbbed and my breath burst before me. My fears were real, my heart quickened with every second I held the tiger in my gaze. But as I stared, I saw nothing of the demon he had come to be.

I felt the breeze touch my cheek as a line of clouds passed before the sun, bringing mottled brown dots down in shadows upon the path.

I thought the tiger seemed so calm, such a peaceful animal. As we faced each other, marking the seconds between us, I lessened the grip on my fear and I soon drew out my deep curiosity.

I could see this animal contained no terror. He had markings which were unusual, which were the tiger's alone, but I knew I was wrong to let my fears rule my head. At once I wished to right my thinking. I wanted to judge the tiger afresh, to see it as it appeared to me now.

The clouds receded and the sun glowed warmly above. The tiger's yellow-tinged coat began to glow, showing the dark gaps in his ribcage. He was a lean animal, strong and sinewy where he stood before me in the path.

Beneath the sun's heavy throb I felt sweat beading on my brows and down my spine. I held myself like a pillar, my heels were deep in the soft ground. My muscles began to ache and twitch from the strain of being so tense and I knew that one of us must soon move.

I took one step beyond where I stood. Slowly, I lowered my hand towards the tiger and then I reached out to him. "Hello, friend," I whispered, "hello, friend."

For a moment, I thought the tiger would come to me, his nostrils widened and flared for the briefest of instants. I reached out further for him. "Yes, I am a friend," I said softly.

But then, quicker than the breeze, the tiger darted.

In a few large bounds the tiger leapt from me, running high into his stride. As I watched, the first and only tiger I had ever seen disappeared into the scrubland.

For a few tense seconds I could not move. This tiger was no ordinary animal, I saw there was magic carried within his sad eyes; hadn't the grey mare and the other animals felt this, too?

"Goodbye, friend," I said. "Goodbye."

My secret surged to get out and I longed to tell my brother Jurgis, but I knew that I could not. I knew I must tell no one, not even Tilly. As surely as my discovery had come to me alone,

I knew I must be the one to hold it back, tighter than the stone walls of a dam.

Though my tiger was gone, vanished into the scrub that lay deep and harsh from path to coast, I still heard his sorrowful cries like an infant. This was the tiger's island, he fought for his ground and claimed this small apple-shaped isle as his own. From the jagged sawtooth tips of the mountain ranges through the rugged gullies and river valleys to the wooded plateaus and button grasses, he roamed free.

My tiger wanted nothing from us. He had all he needed without our flocks and hen coops and wing-clipped geese. And yet, I knew, the settlers still feared him.

Chapter Eight

In the warmth of summer the station fell spiritless.

The grazings were good, they did not dry to the wheat-whites of the main under the hot sun, and the drovers found little work for themselves. Chores like draining waterlogged pastures, or lambing the ewes, looked far away in time. For all the settlers, any flurry of activity became something worth latching upon.

I had just begun baling in the hayloft when I saw the burning in the scrubland at Welcome Heath. I knew at once the scorching of the earth must be something sinister.

Black clouds perched over the land like gargoyles, curling and twisting, contorting their ugly features beneath a blue stretch of sky. The sun gazed on from above, grim and disapproving, directing the gales of wind to carry off the rising spires of smoke before they could come together.

What is happening? I thought.

I threw down my pitchfork and ran straight out into the scrub. I did not know what to expect. I found my legs weak beneath me, folding at my knees as I was carried forward, lightly as a leaf upon the breeze. All around me the air hung heavy and pungent and laced its way angrily into the landscape.

I had not seen the property in such disarray before. At the station store, where the Van Diemen's Company held my family's credit, the closed sign hung on the door; this was the first I had seen of it. The storekeeper stood out front, a short brown boater pulled firm across his brow. He did not look used to sunlight and seemed uncomfortable in the outdoors, but he carried an old muzzle loader in his grasp and strode out to meet the men that stood in the street.

A woman gathered up a red-haired child and called out,

"Quick, the children, get the children indoors!"

The little ones, all about, bawled and screamed. Women bundled them up like packages and rushed them inside, finger-marked and ruddy-cheeked.

"Quick! Quick! Get them inside," the woman wailed on.

Frenzy ran through everyone and a stream of footfalls kicked up a dust storm so thick that I found it difficult to see a yard to the front. Restless leaves rustled all around me and a hundred cries rippled through the air.

"Get out of the way, boy!" I was ordered by a man with a rifle. As he laid his hand on my chest and pushed past me I saw the dry dust caught in his dark whiskers.

I ran recklessly into the confusion, but I was shoved aside again and again. "Myko, get to the billet," said a voice I recognised. It was one of the women who kept my mother's company on wash-day. But I could not see her through the crowds, as my gaze trawled the tight packed hordes I saw only one face I knew for sure.

"Tilly," I called out, "Tilly, over here."

Tilly raised her hand above her eyes to seek out who had made her name. Dust marks clung around her mouth and beneath her nose where she breathed in the heavy foot-spray floating all around.

She could not see me. "Tilly, Tilly … this way," I called out again.

Somehow she sensed where I stood and came running towards me. As Tilly moved she seemed to disappear for an instant and at once I realised she had fallen.

"Tilly," I called as I set out towards her. I waved my arms through the dust but I took only a few steps then I saw her standing again; the patches on her knees looked dark where they broke her fall.

"Myko, what's going on?" she said.

46

I shook my head and drew up my shoulders. "I don't know."

"Something is the matter," said Tilly, "look!" Where she pointed I could see that every man held a weapon, either a rifle or a stiff blue gum waddy; they were all held out front, all at the ready.

"They're worked up about something," said Tilly. "Come on, Myko, follow me."

I felt panic rising from the deep core of me. My legs trembled as a bursting sweep of wind caught my back and propelled me down a shaly road behind Tilly, "Where are we going?" I said.

"There." She pointed to a tree-bordered clearing, I saw metal-grey smoke rising beyond.

"What are they burning?"

"The scrub."

The idea was strange to me. "Why?" I asked.

"They're trying to shift something out of there. Come on, Myko, let's go see."

We ran through the silver tussock plains. Ground larks and galahs screamed in the sky high above us as they fled the burning scrublands. I heard the cracking noise of great trees falling. Dust and smoke rose everywhere and the perfume of eucalyptus carried in the air. My eyes burned red as I saw the bushfire looming ahead.

The game behaved in a frantic manner; wallabies scampered at full pelt from the forest and settled in the earthy tang of the open plains. I felt the blood pumping in my head. I grew dizzy and could not think clearly. All around me the voices of men yelled; it seemed like fine sport to them.

I stopped still and tried to calm myself, to better understand the cries falling all around me. Suddenly, I was stunned, knocked dumb as any possum in a trap, as I heard the word "TIGER" ring out.

Tilly came to a halt a few paces ahead of me. She turned to stare open-mouthed as I took in the yells filling the air; I could tell the appearance of my face startled her.

"Myko, what is wrong?"

I said nothing in reply. For a moment Tilly stared on at me, and then she dropped her head low on her chest and ran towards me. At my side Tilly grabbed my shirtsleeves and shook me where I stood. "Myko … Myko, what's wrong?"

I saw her lips moving but her voice did not register in my ears. I heard only the cries of "TIGER".

"What's going on, Tilly?"

She dropped her arms before me. Tilly's eyes were wide and still as she took me in, and then she turned from me, staring towards the dark depths of the forest. "They have found a tiger, Myko." Tilly's voice came so low and faint that I hardly believed I heard the words.

"What … what did you say?" I roared at her. I spun Tilly around by the shoulders, "What did you say?"

As she faced me, I saw her eyes were moistening, "They have found a tiger," she said once more.

I knew there to be only one tiger in this range. At once I took off, running for the pack of men. Their beast-like howls fell all around. The men returned to their primitive type, the entire station taken up with the rage of the hunt.

Great smiles filled the flushed red faces of the men as they ran through the smoking scrublands. Black soot gathered under their eyes and around the corners of their mouths like the natives' war paints. Roo dogs barked at their heels; they ran wildly as ever, their long jowls frothed white with the exertion of the chase. They scented the tiger and became reluctant to follow, but the men cajoled and pointed front and the roo dogs' terror vanished.

All the while my eyes stung with the smoke and tears spilled down my face, hot as dripping wax.

"Myko. Myko," cried Tilly as I ran, "we should go back."

"Why?" I called out amidst the rising fury.

"Myko, there'll be trouble, the men won't want us here."

I kept to my hard pace and ignored Tilly, but I did not want to see the blue sky open up before us. I did not want to feel the green field grasses beneath my feet once more. When they came, I wished I could lead the wailing pack of men out above the cliff edge, running on only the clearest of air, all the way to the jagged rocks below.

The roo dogs howled bravely as they came first upon the plains. I watched them leap, starting with the first of the men, their eyes gleaming like quartz as they lunged into the day's sunlight once more.

The men's Purdy shotguns, the barrels broken over their arms, were quickly snapped into place as the sun bowed before them. They dropped to their knees and forced down the dogs' snouts, towards the ground, to catch the tiger's scent once more.

"Seek, seek," they called out.

The roo dogs sniffed at the dry grass as if their supper was buried beneath. They knew what they were looking for and there was no doubt they had the scent already.

The dogs kept their heads low, hoping to find a familiar trail, perhaps a black goose or a dusky moorhen, anything but the tiger's fearsome scent. They whimpered, making desperate glances to their masters, but they earned scoldings for their cowardice and were once again forced in upon the task.

"Seek, seek," was roared out now, and this time the dogs gave in to the command. I watched, knowing that my tiger's fate was nearing.

My eyes stung harsh in my head but I dared not shift my gaze from the plains to rub or wipe. Streams of moisture rolled down my face and the light poured out slantwise over the sculptured hills, and the smoke-warped gum branches slid behind me. And then I saw him.

As my painful eyes washed over the scene I knew at once I was the first to see my tiger. Before even any of the baying hounds that took chase firm upon his tail, I had found him.

"Tilly, look there …" I yelled out.

"The tiger!"

I watched my tiger slowly trot across the plains. His legs were short, his body deep-chested and strong. He was not made for speed, but I knew he could run for great distances with his powerful stride.

The black stripes upon his back stood out clearly against the yellow-brown of his coat. My tiger shone in the sun, and the island rolled out beneath him as though it were saluting his every stride.

I watched my tiger chased, pursued by the roo dogs and the ringing of gunfire. I coughed for breath, my lungs nipped in the open air, but I could not be moved from this sight for a second.

I stood beneath the desolate sky and feared for my tiger and then, as I saw him clear a patch of low bushes, my heart suddenly gladdened.

"Quick … faster," called the men. They fired their guns and shouted, "faster … get in there!"

The roo dogs dropped from the chase as the cracking barrels of shotgun fire failed to make halfway upon my tiger's tracks.

"Tilly, he's made it." I could tell my tiger had moved beyond the pack's range.

"He's beaten them, Myko … look, look." Tilly's voice sounded high and excited.

I had believed all was lost but my tiger showed he was the

more cunning. He put distance between his pursuers, enough to let him flee to safety. As the settler's loud uncouth curses fell all around me I felt my spirits begin to sing.

"Damn it … God damn it!" the men cried out.

I prayed my tiger would not return. I prayed he would leave this place and keep far from the doings of the station.

"Tilly, he's made it … he's made it." Together we jumped into the air. Tilly's smile was the greatest sight I had ever seen as she screamed her happiness for all to hear. But then, suddenly, she became still.

Tilly froze before me; the wind caught a curl of her hair and sent it into her eyes but she did not remove it, she merely stared on, set still. "Myko … look," she said.

I followed the tip of Tilly's finger to where she pointed. As I watched my tiger nearing the coastal run and the dunes thick with heavy grasslands where his freedom lay, my blood ran cold.

"No!" I yelled.

I felt my heart begin to weaken and my knees sag beneath me. My eyes could not comprehend the sight unfolding before us. I felt all hope leave me instantly.

"No! No!" I called out.

As I wailed, I watched my father rise from beyond the horizon's thin line and break the sun's rays with his powerful frame. Where I watched my father stand he was granite-spined. He raised up a repeater rifle, turning down his head to place an eye upon the scope mount, and then he dropped my tiger with one shot.

Tilly screamed out as my tiger lost his stride and fell.

My knees folded up beneath me. I saw my tiger, where he lay, had only a few more of his great bounds to take to find his freedom again. But now he rested in the shadow of the dune; the sunlight which had filled him, fled.

He struggled, not quite dead, raising up his large head, but he fell again and again.

"No, Father … no, no, no," I cried.

I closed my eyes tightly and felt a heavy scarring grow upon my heart. And then I heard the rifle shot with which my tiger ceased to be.

I did not dare to put my eyes upon my father below.

Chapter Nine

The storekeeper took off his boater and threw it in the air.

Many hats were raised aloft, but I could not share in their carousing, I knew a great evil had been done this day. As the station's men started towards my father with cheers I felt like I carried my heart within a glass jar, sealed fast to the world outside.

"Myko," said Tilly, "your father has killed a tiger."

I wished to leave this place, to be far from the island.

"I know ... I saw it," I cursed and spat, "he has killed my tiger."

The blood pounded in my temples and I could not stay any longer. I hurled myself back toward the forest.

"Myko, Myko," I heard Tilly call out at my back, but I was running hard; I was already beyond the distance where Tilly could catch me.

Smoke still lingered like thick fog in the forest, but a mist now crept around me. I ran on, spitting out the sooty air as it gathered in my throat. I stumbled and found myself fallen, my hands and knees scratched upon the forest floor.

Ash and charcoal surrounded the gnarled roots of the hardy trees; they resisted the burning beneath them as no more an inconvenience than a bird resting upon their high branches. Quickly I picked myself up, and ran on. The green and blue half-tones of the country became a blur to me as I rushed through the wattles and mud-holes. The smell of burnt eucalypts sailed high on the heavy sea breeze that raked the air and sent the branches twitching. Beneath the desolate sky was an eerie calm as the sun crawled away to hide. I wished I too had somewhere to curl up and extinguish the flames burning inside of me, but I could only run on and on.

By nightfall I grew weary. I did not know how far I had travelled. Feverish new chills passed over me in the cold of the night. I wandered along a tree-bordered road that led I knew not where as the moon rose up like a phantom.

The hazy stars threw down dim lights that landed upon the sag of the road and tethered themselves to each silver beam's fall. In the low humming of the night I watched the island's landscape break up like a mosaic, and then I was suddenly startled to see the bright lights of a motor truck wending its way towards me on the dirt track.

Whistle screams rose from the noisy engine and tore through the silence like a cleaver. The truck was fast approaching as I stepped into the road's culvert, but the lights' shine pinned me where I stood. It did not take long for the cracked and broken earth to be illuminated in the truck's lights, which chased away the darkest of the lurking shadows.

The truck came to rest and from the window leaned a shearer. He eyed me with alarm, tipping back his stockman's hat and staring down upon me. "You're a long way from home," he said; as his crooked front teeth pressed on his taut little mouth his words greeted me like mule kicks.

I did not answer and merely restarted my steps upon the road. There was a bitter taste in my mouth. I believed it to be the words I dared not speak for fear of unleashing torrents which I had no power to control. I did not want to pass time with any of Tasmania's bushmen or fools.

"The name's Ben, I come from Trowutta," said the shearer, opening the truck's door and leaning out to face me.

I stared on for a moment, then returned to the road.

"I can take you to the billet at Woolnorth," he said, "it's where I'm headed."

When the shearer spoke of the billet I suddenly thought of my mother. I knew I must not leave her to face these days alone; she suffered when I was far from her. I wanted to run away but I knew that the absence of another son might be the ending of my mother. I could not have her fragile spirit weakened still more by the island's brutes.

"I'll travel with you," I told the shearer; I hoped my passions would cool.

"What's your name, boy?" he said, once I had settled in the cab.

"Myko."

The shearer looked at me with his red-edged eyes. "What you doing way out here, boy?"

I did not feel like talking to anyone; my words came to my mouth as crisp as new apples. "I was just walking."

"You want to be careful where you walk." As he spoke to me the shearer lowered his voice to a faint hiss and I could see dark pencil lines drawn around the furrows of his face. "There's tigers hereabouts, y'know!"

To hear the shearer speak of tigers made my spine straighten. As I snatched at my reply I felt my lips start to quiver. "What do you know of tigers?"

The shearer took his hand from the wheel for an instant and drew back a dusty tarpaulin which lay between us on the cab's seat. Below, was a crude picture-box. I saw the glass and shining metal of the lens, there was a little bone-coloured handle and three folded wooden legs with brass pintle fasteners.

"You know what this is?" he said.

I nodded. I had seen hawkers carry picture-boxes to the station many times and I saw the settlers pay to have their images captured.

He seemed irritated by my knowledge. "Well, do you know what it's for, boy?" he hollered.

I found the question an odd one; his talk was chipping at my nerves. "For taking pictures," I stated flatly.

Suddenly the shearer brought the truck to a halt; the smell of the engine's smoke came quickly into the cab. "Boy," he addressed me, turning in the cab seat and bringing his face to within a few short inches of my own, "I am on my way to take a picture of the Woolnorth Tiger!"

I watched as a smile played on the corners of the shearer's mouth, his eyes opened wide before me.

"But the tiger is dead," I said.

"Huh?" the shearer blurted. His smile lowered and his lips became as thin as rice-papers.

"The tiger is dead," I said again.

"Well, I know that, boy. Who'd pay money for a picture of it alive? No, sir, I'm going to take a picture, many pictures, dang it, of the tiger and the men who hunted it down." The shearer smiled again. "I hope to make a pretty penny, I can assure you of that."

As he engaged the truck once more, the shearer twitched with excitement, slapping down his hot palm on the steering wheel. "News of the tiger chase spread to Trowutta faster than any bushfire," he said, "when I got word of that shooting I snatched up my picture-box here and headed straight for the truck. Yes, boy, them settlers should earn me a pretty penny!"

The shearer was filled with excitement, he clapped his open palm on the wheel again and seemed dizzy with his prospects. I did not understand his venture: dead, to me my tiger's value was nothing.

As the road wended on, to the tune of overhanging branches tapping on the window, I clamped my jaws tightly. I was determined to hold in the emotion that the shearer's words stoked in me.

He spoke constantly of the tigers. "You know, boy them dang tigers were once abundant in these parts, just about trip over them, you would."

He pulled down the windowpane and spat out into the open air. "Takes a keen tracker and a steady hand to catch them now, though, but them dang tigers roam the whole island and there could be a shifting come our way."

"What do you mean?"

"What I mean, boy, is you just never know when you're gonna be lucky and spot one."

The shearer pointed to the back of the cab, "Look up there."

There was a Marlin rifle above the luggage box. "Just in case I get lucky," he said.

The shearer smiled down on me as I looked at the rifle. "I'd let you take it down for a look, boy, but I keep it loaded."

I remained silent where I sat and I kept my eyes on the road before us; I hoped no tiger presented itself.

"The tiger man at Mount Cameron must have claimed a pretty bounty in his time," said the shearer, bristling with excitement again. "Yes, God damn it, I think the tigers are coming less and less now."

He raised a finger above his head, towards the rifle. "But the bounty paid makes for a handsome billfold. If there is any more on the Van Diemen's Company's ground you can be assured of more hunts raised."

As we travelled my thoughts seemed to gallop before me. I sat as quiet as a stunned quoll; the shearer must have thought me struck dumb by his words.

I watched my worst imaginings play out as the wind slapped at the truck's sides and the night drew on.

I held no end of fears for the tigers now, but as we reached Woolnorth the reality I dreaded most confronted me, worse than any of my imaginings.

Chapter Ten

When the Czar's soldiers were done with our house in the Sakiai, done tearing rugs and curtains and linen, when they were done spearing mattresses with their swords and sending feathers whirling into the air, they surveyed the courtyard where they found Aras, harnessed obediently to Father's cart.

An iron-faced man in uniform took long, heavy strides around the cart. He pulled at the jute ropes securing our possessions.

"Whose cart is this?" said the man. He pulled again at the ropes; they were tied tightly for the long journey ahead of us and the load did not move.

"Whose cart is this?" said the man once more.

My mother sobbed uncontrollably, her shoulders trembled and her eyes grew to look like those of a captive animal. Mother's glance darted between us boys and my father, then, as if struck by palsy, she was still. My mother stood unmoving as she followed my father's approach to the cart and the soldiers.

"Petras," Mother called in a low whisper.

I did not know what to expect as I watched Father's steps. The whole night seemed unreal to me. It was as though I lay awake in my bed, unable to move, trapped in the grip of some terrible nightmare.

Aras raised up his head and my father touched the flash of white that ran along the packhorse's nose, as was their usual greeting.

"This is my cart," said Father.

The iron-faced man said nothing, he merely watched as my father gently stroked Aras. Father and his horse appeared calm, but agitation soon grew on the soldier's face.

"Get me a knife," he called out, "a knife, a knife quickly!"

Heavy soldiers' boots pounded across the courtyard, cracking loudly on the darkened sets beneath.

"Sir," said a young boy in the Czar's uniform; he presented the blade's handle on his arm and lowered his head graciously.

The iron-faced man snatched the knife and quickly cut into the jute ropes. At once Aras raised up his head and pressed into the harness.

"Whoa, now," said Father as the cart rocked, "whoa, whoa."

Suddenly, with a loud noise, our possessions crashed onto the courtyard. The sound of breaking glass startled Aras and he jerked forward, forcing my father to drop the harness and leap to the side.

The iron-faced man laughed loudly and the soldiers followed his lead; the entire mob seemed amused. The riotous laughter startled Aras, his ears twitched nervously as he fetched up his legs and brayed out.

"Down. Down," called the iron-faced man.

As fast as it appeared the laughter stopped, and the man called out again, "Down. Down," he said.

Aras did not respond, and the soldier.drew his pistol.

"No," said Father, "no, no." He leapt before the gun and shielded Aras.

"Get out of my way," yelled the soldier; he raised up his arm, and struck Father across the face with the gun's barrel.

"Petras!" yelled my mother. I felt her fingers tighten around my arm as we watched Father fall to the ground. "Petras, no." I turned to see Mother close her eyes tightly, and then we heard the loud ringing of the gun's discharge.

The bullet went into Aras's thick neck, but did not slow him. He reared up higher, he seemed only to be angered by the shot.

The packhorse gathered his pace and raised gallop in the

courtyard. The soldier fired again and again. Spouts of dark blood sprayed from Aras's neck and belly, but he did not fall.

When more shots were fired the cart overturned throwing out the last of our possessions and Aras lost ground. But still it did not stop our packhorse.

Aras spat breath from his nostrils; it rent the air like steam powering from a locomotive as he turned and charged, loosing himself on the soldier.

In my mind I imagined Aras was able to save us all, but it was not to be.

"Fire. Fire," yelled the iron-faced man.

His soldiers were still as he stood red-faced and butted his pistol to his thigh. "I command you, fire," he yelled once more. As he gave the order to fire a second time his soldiers, in their green uniforms with their rifles raised, brought down our beloved packhorse.

Where he fell, Aras lay, breathing deeply, his huge ribcage rising and subsiding like a distant mountain glimpsed beyond the horizon.

I tried to run to him, but my mother held me back, her nails digging deep white crescents into my arms.

"Aras," I cried, "Aras. Aras. Aras."

I watched Father remove his hat and twist it in his hands; he too wanted to run to Aras, but the soldiers held him back with their rifles and swords.

"Take him," yelled out the iron-faced man, swiping the air with his pistol, and Father was led away, bundled into a large carriage. I looked to my mother to see where the soldiers were taking him, but I could tell she did not know either.

"Petras," screamed my mother as the soldiers closed the carriage doors, "Petras, wait ... please, no."

My mother still held me tightly until, of a sudden, all three of us were lifted up and carried far from our home.

"Quickly, this is no place for you now," said one of the farm women as she bundled us along the path to the forest, away from the soldiers and away from my father.

We walked deep into the forest; our legs ached after crossing such a great distance. By nightfall we slept outside with the women and children from our village.

Our people were too scared to return to their homes. The Czar's army took all the young men. My young brother, Jurgis, sobbed as he clung to my mother, but she spoke little. It seemed as if she, too, was taken, and only a small portion of our mother remained.

We picked mushrooms together in the morning and drank clear, sweet water from a brook. All around us the forest was filled with the wails of women for their husbands and sons.

"What has become of us?" said one woman, "what will we do?"

"We have nothing, they have taken everything," said another, "oh, why, why did they come here now? Why did they not stay in the towns where they can have comfort, where they can take from the wealthy?"

Mother caught me watching the women, she saw me wondering, trying to make sense of their words, and then she covered my ears with her hands and led my brother and me from the forest.

"Where are we going, Mama?" I asked.

"We are going home," said Mother.

I jumped to my feet. I longed to go home, there were many questions which I hoped would be answered on our return.

As we walked, I spoke: "Mama, why did they take Papa?"

Mother raised a hand to her mouth, as if trying to hold something back. She raised her hand to her head and swept back her long black hair, which she neatly put behind her ear, then continued in her stride. She had no words for me.

A little further down the trail I tried again. "Will he come back to us?" I asked. But again, my mother did not answer.

Once we returned home my mother laid out food for my brother and I and then she left us alone. We ate quietly together. Neither of us dared to mention what we had seen, but I knew Jurgis shared my fears.

"We should find Mama," said my brother when we were finished eating our food.

We left the table and set about the house looking for our mother. When we found her, she was in her bedroom, lain upon the floor. Our father's clothes were strewn about her, her face beneath a favourite shirt of his. There was a photograph, taken on their wedding day, clasped in her hands.

My brother looked searchingly at me for an answer, but I shrugged back at him. We both knew not to speak, so I crouched down beside Mother and gently touched the back of her head. There was no movement from her. She was so still, like a felled tree.

"What is wrong?" whispered Jurgis, tugging on my shirtsleeve.

"I don't know."

"Is she sick?"

"I don't know."

"Is she asleep?"

I had no answers for my brother, I was as perplexed as he was by the sight before us.

"Perhaps, she is asleep," I said finally.

I leaned forward and touched my mother's face; she felt warm. I moved closer to my mother and lay beside her on the floor, at her back; as I did so I felt my brother join us.

And so we lay with Mother on the floor, curled up like her cubs, succumbing to new ways we had yet to learn of.

Chapter Eleven

I never expected such fanfare upon my return to the billet. Lights blazed and fiddles played as the shearer smiled and removed his sweat-brimmed hat, then took to wiping down his teeth with a piece of rag. "Come on now, boy," he said, shaking out the rag, "there's a time to be had."

The shearer glowed with the excitement of the night. His steps fell jauntily as his heels tapped over the stone path.

"Help me get set up with this picture-box," he said, "now be careful, there's a pretty penny to be made with this piece of tackle!"

I held up the picture-box and watched him unfurl the wooden legs and straighten them with their brass pintle fasteners.

"Listen up," he said, curling his hand around the back of his ear, "sounds like quite a crowd." He smiled widely, showing the fine job he'd made of cleaning his teeth.

"Well, come on, boy." He placed a hand upon my back and shook me where I stood. "Now try not to look like it's the gallows you're headed for!"

I strode on quietly, my eyelids lowered as I gulped down my emotions and made towards the thick snubbing post of the door.

Great merriment and activity filled the billet, the mood had lifted, but it did not reach me. At once my attention turned to a new presence: I smelled the scent of my tiger. Its strong musk rent the air like firecrackers; there was no mistaking my tiger's closeness.

I looked around, but I could not see him. My mind was all a scatter as my gaze flooded the broad room. *Where was my tiger?* Faces burst from every corner of the barn. Bright faces, blooms set on their cheeks, polished brows shining in the firelight.

Laughter rose all around me and voices sounded high in mirth beside the strings of fiddles. I trained my eyes to the lantern-light; my stares cut through the haze of warm bodies and heady spirits, and then, finally, I saw him.

"No," I said aloud. I turned away, but was drawn back again.

My tiger was stretched lifeless across Father's lap. A pewter tankard atop his skull spilled stout down upon his crown in dark rivers.

I wanted to run out. I wanted to throw my head in the water trough and cool my brows, but suddenly I heard my name called.

"Myko! Myko!" I watched as my mother picked up her skirts and ran to me.

Her eyes looked pale and tired, but could not hide the jolt in her emotions. "Myko, Myko," she said, her mouth quivering on every word, "I was so worried about you!"

My mother held me, tight as a saddle-belt, where I stood. "My Myko, you have come back to me." I saw her spirits rise, as surely as cream rises to the surface of a milk-pail, but then, suddenly, her voice changed. "What is this?" Her eyes were glassy as she took in the sight of the shearer carrying his picture-box.

"Do you think he will allow it, mam?" he said.

The shearer set down his kit and tried to spot my father through the gathering. A spry old woman blocked his way as she stood on an apple box to better view the goings. People I did not know arrived in streams and peach-cheeked children ran amok everywhere.

People in the crowd carried gifts for my father and reached out with hands for him to shake. Below his feet I spied a honey pot and a new woollen blanket; a haunch of beef from the

64

store was roasting upon the open fire.

"I can hardly see a thing," said the shearer, "how am I to take pictures like this?"

My mother pushed me before her and broke into a stride; as she did so she turned to the shearer and said: "I will lead the way."

The shearer smiled widely once more; already I was tiring of his gleaming teeth. "And I will most surely follow," he said, "I will follow."

As we crossed the tight-packed room Father nodded to us and drew my tiger closer to him. His square jaw was held firm, his dark eyes were as black as sea-rocks. My father saw me but did not call me to him; he merely basked in the crowd of adoring eyes which surrounded him.

"Sir, if I may, a few pictures?" said the shearer.

"Yes, pictures, of course," said Father.

The shearer positioned his picture-box and motioned towards my father's lap, where my tiger lay. "Sir, the beast – it must be prominent."

My father let out a playful growl and in one mighty sweep of his arms, lifted my tiger upon his chest.

The lifeless body fell limp in my father's hands, its head lolling slowly, and then Father raised the corpse towards the roofbeams. He moved my once beautiful tiger like a child's toy stuffed with rags, until he had his trophy high enough for all to see.

The crowd cheered as the shearer snapped his first picture of Father with my tiger. It scalded my heart to remember how I had once seen the animal roam free.

"Tuppence a time," said the shearer, "tuppence is all for your very own picture with the Woolnorth Tiger!"

Many sprang upon the offer, but my father bridled, raising his hand quickly and slicing it down like the sweep of an axe.

"No!" he growled; his voice was loud and resonated powerfully. I saw he had no desire to share his prize with anyone.

"But, sir," said the shearer, bowing low to better face my father, "for each picture taken, one penny shall be paid to you."

My father's hard mouth widened to a pearly gleam and then he slapped his hand on his thigh. "We have a deal," he said, as he gripped the shearer's hand tightly.

"Well, I will be first to take up the offer," said one of a pair of fisherman, "we missed the hunt but we'll have a picture as a minding of this day … ain't often we see a tiger taken now."

Where the fishermen stood before my father their faces clouded with awe. I watched the first fisherman hand my father a bucket of eels as a mark of respect and approval.

"Thank you," said my father, "I have use for such things." I knew Father was pleased by the gifts he received; for so long we had so little.

Where the fishermen stood they rocked on their sturdy boot-heels with their heads lowered. They seemed trapped by a web of embarrassment, but their happiness to please my father glowed as hot as the belly of a stove.

The taller of the two seemed eager to address my father. He stepped forward and made a great show of throat clearing to signal his intention to speak. When his words broke a tremor rose in his voice.

"I-I once came across a bull tiger," said the fisherman. He removed his felt hat and smoothed down his pale fringe, "as big as a full grown man it were … I swear he stood over five feet tall!"

My father and the people around him listened with great interest. As the fisherman spoke, a hushed awe filled the billet. It grew so quiet that I heard the soft spray of raindrops on the windowpanes; outside the river's current rang strong and deep and clean.

"I was walking back from McCabe's Paddock when out the wattle there he stood." The fisherman ran his tongue over his scaly lips as he spoke. "He had a lamb in his great jaws, I believe he was draining its blood as I come upon him. Well, the tiger saw me and there was a growl came out him. I swear I wasn't game to tackle him, I had no weapon on me save my bare hands."

Every face in the barn fixed upon the fisherman. As he lowered his voice hardly a sound was made, save the rustle of clothing and the creak of boards as people leaned closer, careful not to miss a word.

"As I watched that bull tiger, I stood rigid," he said, "and then, God strike me blind if this is a word of a lie, but another came upon me. It were his mate, she were smaller by a full two feet of length, but she were maddened by me. She leapt for my throat, but I had the chance to grab a rock up from beneath me and make a lob at her as she sailed through the air. That useless slut fell faster than any penny in a well. Them are the most useless animals in the bush, I swear!"

"But what about the bull?" called out one of the children.

"I was coming to that, yes sir, I were. The bull no more cared I'd killed his mate than he could imagine a pig with wings in the sky above us. He kept his big eyes on me, but the lamb was his main concern, he were sucking its blood as natural as any lamb suckles to its mother. It were as right as the day to him, but to me it were a sight. I think I must have grown my confidence when I took down his slut for I leapt for him and we had us a wrestle there and then upon the dirt. There was blood dripping from his fangs but I was a man in no mood to be scared by such things. I was ready to kill that brute stone dead."

"Did he bite you?" It was the same child again.

"No, my little one, he did not," said the fisherman

enthusiastically, "I was reaching my hands around his throat. I would have strangled him where he lay, but the beast took fright and ran from me. The last I saw of him was when he took off running through the wattle. I swear he moved faster than any terrier taking for a rabbit hole."

"What did you do with the mate?" said the child.

"I took her up to the hut with me; she had young in her pouch, that's the reason she was so set to kill me. A tiger slut will always attack when carrying young, y'see. I did plan to raise the pups and claim a bounty on them when they were full grown, but my kangaroo dogs killed them before they were another day old. The slut, I got a whole pound for, and ten shillings for each the pups."

"Did you keep the skin, can we see it?" said the child. He had consumed every word of the fisherman's story; I knew sleep would be a trouble to him this night.

"No. No, I didn't keep the skin."

"Why not?" said the other fisherman. He squared his shoulders beneath his tweed coat and pushed forward his square-clipped beard. "How come I never heard you talk of no tiger before?"

"I just didn't keep it, that's all. I knew a fella once bought them up, he sold them to another fella who sent them to London, said they were all the rage for the gentlemen's waistcoats. I think there was tailors waiting on them skins, got them by the thousand. But mine were a mite on the raw side, I had no desire to keep that smelly beast's coat around as a reminder."

Fever gripped everyone inside the billet; the people were raised on such fare as this all their lives and now they had their very own tale to tell. But I could not suffer their voices a second more and I slipped into the shadows towards my bunk.

As I left the crowd I stumbled, knocking over a mop handle. When it landed it jolted my nerves, and my blood rushed faster.

I felt cruelly punished as I stumbled onto my bunk and covered my ears to all the noise within the billet.

I begged for sleep to take me far from this world, but as I lay awake I was alive to every board's creak.

Chapter Twelve

The morning after the billet had celebrated the killing of my tiger, fierce quarrels raged within our large and open barn.

A woman screamed at the top of her lungs for a missing sliver of soap. Another let wail about the few flakes of mouldy flour she received in her rations.

"Out, you drunken whore," cried the factor, as he grabbed a woman from her bunk.

"Go to hell!" she roared at him.

"I'll give you hell," said the factor as he raised a cane and brought it down on the woman's back. She roused enough to lunge at him, biting his thigh.

"Whore!" called out the factor and swiped the cane across her gullet.

The woman fell back on her bunk and groaned loudly. The factor dragged her by her long, greyed hair to the door and as they went the woman coughed blood, before she was cast upon the road. Her children, still in their nightshirts, followed weeping at her heels.

"Stay clear, stay clear, you hear!" said the factor as he made to slam the door on them.

The station workers and their wives were of a coarser kind than I had known. Our own people were a mild and accepting lot, but the Tasmanians were of wilder stock.

As I ran to the window to watch the family that the factor had turned out, my attention shifted quickly. A shower of young boys swarmed around the front of the barn where Father had nailed my tiger.

"A shilling, a shilling," said the biggest of the boys to every passer-by, "one shilling and you may touch its hide!"

I turned back to the barn where I joined my mother by

the fireside. The warm glow unfurled a golden rug beyond the hearthstone. As Mother turned her face to me, her coal-black hair shone bright. "Myko, what is wrong? You look so fearful, tell me and I will help."

I did not know what to say or how to answer her. I knew there was nothing she could do. Since my father had brought down my tiger I felt as helpless as ever, more helpless even than when the Czar's soldiers arrived in the Sakiai. At least then I had hopes my father would protect us, but now it was my father who stoked my fears.

Mother picked up one of the bulging candle mounds and scraped the wax into an old tin can. "Do you know when you were newborn we had a beautiful life," said Mother as she placed the can at the fireside.

She sighed heavily. "Yes, we had a beautiful life then … what has happened to us, Myko?"

I looked up at her, her eyes were wistful as she stared into the warmth of the flames; I felt my mother shared my fears.

"I don't know what has happened, Mother."

"No, and nor do I!" She threw down the tin. The wax scrapings spilled on the boards at her feet.

"Do you know, in the old country, when you were born, Myko, we were so blessed that people then believed we owned a returning coin!"

Mother smiled, and I began to laugh.

"It is true … it is true," she said. "Do you know what a returning coin is, Myko?"

"No, I don't."

I had never heard of such a thing. It was strange to hear my mother talking of the old country. It seemed so very far away, such a different place to where we were now.

As my mother placed her tired eyes upon me they flickered

71

in the fire's light. She seemed happy to think of the old country and our old ways like this; I believe she too felt her spirits sickening within this place.

"A returning coin, Myko, is a very special coin – one that returns to you whenever something is bought."

I felt my eyes widen. "Anything?"

My mother leaned forward, she dipped her head and smiled. "Anything! You could buy goods from a store and it would make its way back – that is a returning coin!"

She clasped her hands together; her happiness seemed to fill the room. "Yes, my Myko, in the Sakiai for a time, they believed we possessed such a thing."

My mother began to laugh, creases were formed at the side of her mouth and around her eyes, thin little lines I had never seen before which were illuminated by the firelight.

"And do you know," she said, "such a coin also brought back all the money a person ever possessed? Yes, my Myko, surely someone who possessed such a coin enjoyed a beautiful life indeed. No?"

I nodded. "Yes, Mama."

"But, now we have no such coin. If we did, it is gone."

My mother smiled again. She held me to her by the fire. I was glad to be back by her side, I knew then that my mother's love was something I would never lose. Though I sensed we had all lost so much already, I knew my mother would always stay by my side. The thought was a great comfort to me as my father appeared in the doorway before us.

"Myko," he called out, "gather yourself, we have much to do today."

My father sounded harsh, I dreaded seeing him. I could hardly bear to place my eyes on him without feeling a burning anger rising in my guts.

"Myko," said Father, "to the cart at once!"

My mother pushed me away. "Quick. Go. Do as your father says."

I raised myself and ran past my father, straight through the doorway.

With the young Scotsman, Nathaniel, we took a slow trail to the southern hills creek. The road made a small rise beneath the black-wet spiles of the bridge where the mud-brown waters lapped high after the heavy rains.

The sun stretched over the paddocks where long blue shadows reached out from the gum-tree bases. The horses' breath came heavy in the dense air and all around spread the fresh tang of steam rising from the wattle grasses.

As we travelled along the road's small rise, Nathaniel stroked the checkered walnut stock of his bolt action Winchester. "A fine selector's firearm," he said, "just fine … just fine."

Nathaniel sat silently for some moments as he admired the Winchester, and then he sat bolt upright, his eyes popping.

"I will shoot me a tiger," he blurted, "and it better be soon."

Nathaniel lifted the gun up and fired off a single shot into the scrub. The rifle crack nearly slung him from the carriage – his shoulder was not firm enough to hold the recoil.

"I swear, I will shoot me a tiger!" he shouted.

The breeze carried the smell and taste of gunshot but Father was silent as he watched Nathaniel lower the rifle. In my mind I raked the air with my fist and brought it down on Nathaniel's pointed nose, but I held myself in check and did not move an inch.

I watched as the lavender hills pulsed on the horizon and the sunlight continued to ooze over the land. My anger had been stabbed and my blood was up; I knew it would take little to see me vent my emotions this day.

At the creek there had been heavy rainfall and the

sedgeland covering the hills was stripped, carried down into floodplains below. Stranded lambs stood bleating with fear and terror, while their mothers kept watch over swathes of rippling grey waters, where once their grazings lay.

"The lambs, Myko," said Father, "go and fetch them."

Father rounded up the trembling newborns, carrying them by their hinds two or three in each of his great hands. I helped by chasing after the most spirited ones, returning with them in my arms.

The creatures were a robust breed and struggled with me as I walked, but I soon had them packed tightly together in the cart, behind its close fitting wooden palings.

"Stay with Nathaniel," Father told me, "I will go to fetch the lambs from the low grounds."

I nodded to my father, as Nathaniel moved before me to speak.

"Don't you worry, we'll keep this mob secure," he said, "don't you worry."

Nathaniel's presence vexed me. His talk ranged from killing tigers to how my father would be handsomely rewarded when the Van Diemen's Company bursar came to assign the bounty of one pound. With each new word he spoke I turned further inward, with nothing there to see but a dark pot of bile cooking away.

"You have done a good job," said Nathaniel. "You have done a good job, but you have much to learn."

His words scratched at me. I did not wish to hear any more from him this day.

Nathaniel raised his brows and there was a flash of tawny teeth beneath his hawk-like nose. "Boy, do you hear?"

I fixed him with a glower, I caught his eyes and held them squarely, but my gaze soon lowered and fell to rest on the pocket of his sun-faded shirt. He was older and stronger, and knew he held advantage on me.

Nathaniel approached me, scowling and as prickly as a thistle. "I did not have an answer from you, boy."

As my elder he sensed it was his duty to keep me beneath him in shame and disgrace, but I would not submit to him.

I stared up at Nathaniel again; where he stooped over me he placed his hand on my shoulder and dug his fingers into my flesh. "Them lambs is ready for mulesing," he said.

I did not know what he meant; I still had many words to learn.

"Well, what you waiting for, boy?" he roared at me.

I saw the thin bristles around his mouth turn up like thorns. His fingers clutched my shoulder tighter and then he flung me towards the stock. "Go and get them, and be hasty about it!"

I stumbled towards the cart, my legs carried me quickly but soon gave way beneath me. As I dropped to the road I put out my hands to break my fall, but I was too slow – I landed square on my face. Wet black dirt jumped into my eyes and the salty taste of blood came to my lips.

Nathaniel watched me with a fleer on his face. "Them lambs won't jump down themselves," he said, "go and get 'em!"

Nathaniel walked towards me, pulling a set of hand shears from out his swag. They were old, not yet rusty but long since past their shining best. I lay beneath him and watched as he sharpened the shears on a large flat boulder, making scores along its surface with both sides of the blades.

Nathaniel glided his thumb along the shears' edge. He appeared to be unsatisfied with the result and proceeded to work them in his hand.

He ran the open shears through his thick head of hair several times, trying to gain some oil on the hinge. "Will do another year," he said, squinting at the shears. "Now, you bring me down a lamb there, boy, we'll fix them one at a time."

I raised myself up from the ground; I felt dazed and my mouth throbbed in pain as I did what he told me, and lifted up a lamb.

It struggled in my arms, opening up its mouth and bleating so hard its grey-pink tongue turned to red. I looked at the lamb and back to Nathaniel; I did not want to let it free but my thoughts were swimming as I heard more of Nathaniel's shouts.

"Well, don't just stand there watching the beast whimper," he said, "get it down before me! Get it down!"

As I took down the lamb, my mouth filled with blood. Nathaniel watched me walk with the lamb in my arms; I saw he was impatient as he tapped the open shears against his folded arm.

A magpie cawed out in the air above my head as I reached the end of my trail and, quickly, Nathaniel grabbed the lamb from my arms and spun it headwise between his thighs. "Now watch up, boy, mulesing's a job I had pat when I were your age." With one swipe of the shears Nathaniel lopped off the lamb's tail. I watched it fall at my feet; there was a spout of dark red blood followed where it fell.

The lamb let out a wail and I felt the pain of it sear through my heart. I stood still in the soil. I could not move. I could not even blink my eyes.

Nathaniel continued to hold tightly to the lamb; blood covered his hands as he fumbled under the tail's stump and raised a fold of skin. I watched him slice into the flesh twice more to make a bloody V-shape below the lamb's tail.

As he worked Nathaniel kept up a chatter about his task, but I listened more to the lamb's cries. I felt the animal's pain inside me, but it did not reach me like a board's nail through my foot, it was a heartscald, a deep anguish.

I watched the lamb's blood flowing and knew it to be the same as the blood I tasted in my mouth. I felt as much a part of that lamb's injury as the bloodied rump and seared flesh before me; I decided then to make the Scotsman pay.

Chapter Thirteen

Nathaniel dropped the lamb before him and its hind legs fell from under it. The lamb's wails were endless, they jarred my senses as I watched, biting down hard and tightening my jaw. Where the lamb slumped on the ground it lay motionless, until Nathaniel kicked at it and screamed, "Scat! Stop your whimpering."

The small, weak animal tried to raise itself on its hinds, but could only drag them along behind it on the ground. It took refuge by the roadside, moving only as far as its exhausted frame could carry it from its tormentor.

"I said scat," called Nathaniel, kicking out at the lamb again.

The streaks of blood and shrill bleats stabbed at my heart where I stood under the brassy sun's glare. I felt the wind rippling over the yellow gorse and heard the stream gushing within its low banks, but my mind now wandered far from this place.

As I turned away from the bloody sight which haunted me as surely as a ghost, I thought of one thing: I would make Nathaniel suffer as surely as he had made this creature suffer.

"Did you hear me, boy?" He scolded me with his harsh breath-heavy growl. I turned to face him and caught sight of his twisted mouth hanging like a piece of grizzle. "Them lambs surely aren't going to walk down here by themselves, now, are they?" He laughed loudly to himself. His thin neck quivered like a reed on top of his rocking shoulders and then he added, drolly, "Walk down by themselves, that's not very likely."

As I moved away from him I felt myself growing bolder. I took up the bolt action Winchester and drew steady on its stock. I had never pulled the trigger on any firearm before, but as surely as I drew my breath I was ready to pitch a bullet in Nathaniel's black heart.

My gait was slow and trembling, the gun was heavy in my hands. It was wrong to kill a man, I knew it, but surely God must be on my side.

I watched as Nathaniel stood before me, a second lamb held within his hateful grasp. I still heard the first lamb's bleatings from the roadside where it cried out in agony by the cover of an uprooted tree.

Nathaniel smiled, he was readying himself for his task.

I felt the sun hot on the back of my neck and it chimed with the flames burning inside of me. Where was his pleasure? In the act? In the suffering? My rage spilled over and I let off the gun.

I felt a lightning bolt strike at my shoulder and I was splayed upon the ground, scattered about like a bucket of fire ash. My ears rang from the gunshot, I smelled the powder, I tasted it in my throat.

Nathaniel stood stock-still, his face rigid with fear. His breathing ceased and then he spun sharply and lifted up his hands; I had not hit him with my shot.

I raised myself quickly and, taking up the gun, steadied my aim for a second time. The lamb Nathaniel held between his thighs dropped on its head and quickly righted itself, running for cover in the scrublands.

"Now, boy, don't you be playing games with me," Nathaniel whimpered. The colour left his face as quickly as a mist rising on the back of a gale. In the clear pale sunshine he stood as white as a summer's cloud.

I said nothing, only walked closer and bettered my aim on his heart.

"Now look here, I have no quarrel with you boy. What is

it? Is it the lamb?" Nathaniel's desperate eyes, black as soot, bored into me with their pleas.

I held my mouth firmly closed. I did not listen to the fast stream of his words. My mind was shut to the outside world as tight as the grip of any clamp-vice.

"Boy, I tell you the lambs need doing, they do, they do ..." his voice was quaking, great gaps spread between his faltering words, "the lambs ... they get dags ... they do ... and and ... the dags, they attract the blowflies ... to their hinds."

I did not listen. I knew from his actions that I had brought him nearer to his death rattle than ever he was, but I was unmoved. Phantoms controlled my actions and drove me on.

"And and ... the maggots, they get in ... and there grows festering. We do it so they can survive in the heat of summer. Oh, Lord, child have mercy, please don't kill me ... Don't kill me!"

Nathaniel began to cry. I watched the tears spill from his eyes and his lower lip curl down towards his chin. He was like they call the little tackers, as lost and as frail inside as any infant.

As I watched this pitiful sight unfold I knew he had been broken and paid, yet I was still ready to be his final judge. I clasped the trigger a second time. I held no doubt within me that I would kill him, as I squeezed my finger, and saw the bolt fly up towards the Winchester's prow.

The gunshot cracked and this time I readied myself to be thrown upon the ground, but though my feet leapt, I did not fall. I felt gripped as tight as barrel hoops around my chest and arms, the firearm grasped far out of my reach.

My father let me struggle until I tired and then he lowered me from his grip. I watched him walk away from me where I fell, exhausted.

Father stared at the blood-red lamb as it dragged its

painful hinds, in retreat from its misery, towards the cover of the uprooted tree, then he looked down on Nathaniel, where he sat shaking like a gum branch in a storm.

No words left my father's mouth.

Chapter Fourteen

Droving sheep in the island's winter came as no pleasant chore, I found, as we took the road back to Woolnorth with the southern flocks.

The sun receded quickly and storm clouds crashed against the steep fall of the cliffs, pouring out their loads. The rain washed nut-brown rivulets through the long grasses, to the stony rise of the road. As the road swung through the rocky outcrops, skirted by the naked pasture, the waters swept fast and turned the road to a shallow, muddy stream, and our progress became near impossible.

The rain followed us all along the way. I was doused as well as any clam. My clothes clung to me as clear as wet leaves on a whitewashed paling. But I thought nothing of these miserable conditions; I knew I had wronged far beyond any ordinary punishments and I would soon be made to pay.

My father kept in silence; my actions were a mystery to him. He did not look at me. Even Nathaniel kept his gaze from falling on me, swinging his legs over the cart's side and staring off into the far distance. I knew there would be no more bullying chides from him after the incident with the gun, but I had paid a dear price for such a small freedom.

"Myko," called out my father, "the gate is ahead of us." His voice sounded blunt and carried no hint of emotion.

I jumped down from the cart and ran into the rain to unclasp the knotted rope on top of the gate and the fencepost. I dragged the heavy gate, digging my heels into the wet ground and gritting my teeth tightly.

The ground was heavily rutted but I secured the gate behind a large boulder and began to lead the flocks through, checking all the while for stray lambs.

"Go, go … quick, quick," I called out. As I watched the flocks I stole glances at my father, to be sure I had done as he asked.

My actions with the Winchester rifle had sent poisonous fishes swimming under my skin and now, each time I looked upon my father, they came up to feed. I watched him where he sat, heavy-shouldered, leading the cart through the gate. "Tie the rope tightly," he yelled out.

"Yes, Father."

I did as he said.

"You are sure the rope is tight?" Father called back to me.

I tugged at the rope's knot to show it was held firm and I received a wave to return to the cart once again.

The sky fell to the palest of blues as the road dropped into a deep gulch, backed by grey-black hills. A long stony slope led to a grassy basin and the steep gradient of the road made hard work for the horses.

As we travelled on my father called to me again, "The cartwheels, Myko, below us you must free the cartwheels."

I dropped from the cart and struggled to loose the cartwheels where they had stuck fast, near a foot-deep in the boggy land.

I looked up and saw Nathaniel resting his back on the flat of the cart's floor; where he lay, belly-up, catching the steady rainfall in his mouth, I could see the rise and fall of his Adam's apple as he quenched his thirst.

Father lashed at the horses' backs. "Use both of your arms, Myko," he called out, "both arms."

I saw concern in my father's face, he feared the cart would become trapped, but I did not have the strength to raise the cartwheel. I felt my head fall.

A hearty laugh rang out and as I looked up I saw Nathaniel sitting bolt-upright, watching me struggle in the muddy wheel tracks. I wished to slap him down to size once more, but I would not give in.

I pressed my full weight and strength towards the cartwheel. My grip held firm, but the sodden loam beneath my feet gave no purchase and the wheel slipped back in its track.

"Myko," called out my father.

I continued to struggle and the darkness of the fast approaching night came down around me as fast as a candle coughs out its last spit of wick. "Myko," called my father again, "raise the lanterns."

As I loosened my grip, my father and Nathaniel lowered themselves on the trail to free the cartwheels from the sodden track.

I watched them from beyond the lanterns' glow, until the wheels were slipping easily beneath the cart.

"Myko, bring the water," said Father.

I ran from the cart with the drinking canister and filled a tin cup for Father and myself.

"And a cup for Nathaniel."

As I handed Nathaniel my drinking cup he grinned widely. I returned to the cart to be alone.

We soon took up our journey again. The dark night became filled with Nathaniel's talk, my father's broken replies, and bursts of laughter. I kept my place in the rear of the cart and edged from their company as we trundled over the stony rises and soggy flats of the road.

Soon we drew near to the billet at Woolnorth and I felt sure my mother would run to greet me, but my first sight of her proved me wrong.

By the boundary fence, Mother twitched and trembled under her heavy shawl. I saw two thin lines pinched between her brows. Her eyes, which gave no recognition, held red veins in their rims. She seemed at once to be as frail as a shadow.

My father jumped down from the cart and ran to her with long strides. "Daina, what is it?" he said, placing his arms around her to calm her movements.

Mother did not answer, her conduct appeared cold. She seemed as distant as the far rippling sea.

"Myko," my father called to me, "you must take your mother inside to the fire."

I felt my mouth drooping open. I knew that work awaited us with the new flock. "But, I must help with the keel." The flock needed to bear the station's red ochre stain, every man was pressed to assist; I felt deep shame to be denied this chore.

"Myko," said Father, his voice heavy and certain, "you will go with your mother and sit by the fire." As he placed his dark eyes upon me, I knew I could not refuse his words.

Inside the barn I sat with my mother by the fire. The hearth hissed and spat as I placed a new split log on the embers and a curl of clean smoke rose up.

A sticky heat crept all around us, but my mother did not seem to notice as she gripped the border of her shawl. It once was the whitest of cotton but was now as grey and frayed as the jute rope of the station bell.

To see my mother this way came as a fresh hurt to me. I had not seen her look so forlorn since the Czar's soldiers took my father from us.

"The bursar is coming," said Mother, "to pay your father for his tiger kill."

"Yes," I said, "I have heard Nathaniel talking of him."

Mother's voice dropped low. "You don't approve, Myko?"

I said nothing.

"I can tell you don't," she said. "It does not matter, they say the tigers are a pest, but ..."

The fire crackled loudly in the billet, it sent chinks of light dancing in my mother's eyes. For a moment this appeared to be the only movement she made.

"I remember the dead cuckoo you found, Myko," she said, "and I told you the story of Gegute. You did not like it, but you were very young. Do you remember?"

I did not like to think such a tale once upset me so much. "We can never hunt or shoot a cuckoo, they are special birds," I said.

"That is right, once the cuckoo was a young maiden, a sister of nine brothers whose family name was Kukaichiai. Her first name was Gegute, which means cuckoo, and her nine brothers all went to war, where they were killed in battle."

I remembered the story, the brothers were brave soldiers.

"When her brothers were killed Gegute turned into a speckled bird," said Mother, "and she went to look for her brothers in the deepest woods. She called their names, and she kept on calling them, all through the day, and all through the night. To this day she still calls them."

I continued the tale, "And because she is so busy searching for her brothers, she has no time left to care for her own children. She leaves them to the care of other birds."

We sat in silence for a long time, until Father returned from the keel. I expected him to be agitated, concerned by my mother's condition, but instead, he brought in the bursar with him.

The station's bursar was an official man who wore a black suit of clothes and a tie, his hair combed back high above his forehead. He arrived in a shining black motor car and carried papers in a leather satchel. His appearance brought much excitement in the billet and a small crowd gathered round my father to be sure they were within earshot.

"'Tis a fine beast you caught," said the bursar to my father, "a fine beast indeed."

My father nodded once, a brief nod to recognise the

compliment. As he did so the bursar held out an envelope which he presented with a rising boom in his voice. "The company is always glad to reward its workforce for solid duty," he said, "I know you deserve that, but ..."

My father's smile slipped away and his eyes widened on the bursar where he stood. I knew he had followed every word of the official man's speech, but he did not know what to expect next.

"But, well, there are rumblings that the government doesn't agree with the threat the tigers pose to the company. Did you know the bounty could be gone in a year?"

"I did not," said Father.

"Some think the tigers are becoming scarce."

I watched my father's brow become lined and fretful. He fingered nervously at the envelope in his hands.

The bursar spoke: "We need to act, sir." He reached into his satchel and removed a thin sheaf of papers. "I have a contract here for a tiger man we need in Mount Cameron's west. I see no reason why the job shouldn't go to you ... if you want it, that is."

My father looked stunned; his face was a long white board. His mouth was a dark hammer-blow which cruelly marked his surprise.

Father reached out to the papers that were held before him and then drew them tentatively within his grasp.

I watched the bursar fasten the buckle on his satchel and begin to walk back to his motor car. "Well, that's agreed. I can fill you in on the finer points some time later."

He took short steps, his fine leather heels clicking on the wooden boards as he went. Outside the barn door the bursar glanced back to my tiger. "A grand beast you shot there," he said, "a grand beast indeed."

I felt my father's eyes fall on me as he lowered the papers, but I did not meet their gaze. As I watched the bursar close the door on the shining black motor car and drive away, I heard my tiger's cries come pounding in my head again.

The room's colours flooded into me and quickly turned to white chalk spots before my eyes.

I felt a panic rising in my chest. I knew I was torn inside because I despised the blood on my father's hands. I quickly turned, showing him my back, and ran out for the coastal heathlands. I heard my father calling out to me as I went, but I knew I must get far away from this place.

As I ran, faster and farther from my home, I saw for the first time that my tiger's tragedy was also my tragedy.

Chapter Fifteen

With our mother gone to us, my brother Jurgis and I began the work of our farm in the Sakiai by ourselves.

We took milk from goats, collected eggs and gave fresh straw to the hens. The work brought colour to my brother's cheeks, I could see the white of his teeth and the pink of his gums as he smiled at me.

We both worked hard, we were glad to be given over to such tasks and by nightfall we rested, tired but content. As we lay in our beds, waiting for our hard earned sleep, our minds raced with the new labours and what we must attend to next.

"Myko," said Jurgis, "we still have lots of work to do."

I knew at once what it was he spoke of: the flocks were neglected. "We cannot do everything at once, Jurgis."

"But …" he replied, then he hesitated for a moment; "the flocks, what will become of them?"

"I don't know."

My brother kept silent for a long time and then, very softly, his familiar voice came through the night air. "Our father would know what to do."

His words prodded me like sharp little needles; I did not wish to hear such thoughts brought into the open.

I tried to point Jurgis's mind elsewhere. "We must do our best," I said, "Mother needs us to do all we can."

"Yes, Myko, we must do all we can."

But there was only so much we could do; with our mother and father both lost to us, or so it seemed, the farm work felt like a heavy burden we struggled to share between us.

The wolves howled in the forests that fell around the farm and we spent a restless night.

"It is the wolves again, Myko," said my brother.

"Yes. I hear them. Go back to sleep."

"But the flocks, they may threaten the flocks."

I knew the wolves would soon scatter the flocks. Father said they picked off the weakest first, like the lambs. When they grew bolder they sought out the larger beasts to feed their hunger. "Jurgis, go back to sleep!" I roared.

When the wolves' baying became louder I felt my brother trembling beneath his blankets.

"Jurgis," I called out to him, "there is nothing for you to fear, we are safe … we are behind locked doors."

"The wolves cannot come through doors," he said.

"That is right."

He seemed settled, there was no noise from him for a long time, and then he spoke up: "Only soldiers can find us," he said.

I had no more words for my brother. What could I say to such fears? What could I do?

The very next morning, our worries were taken from us when a strange man and woman arrived at our door. They were brought by a Russian, an official man who wore a dark suit of clothes. He rode in a military carriage and carried papers bound up in a leather scroll.

The man and woman stood behind the Russian and did not speak. Their clothes were old and worn. The man wore patched trousers hitched with a length of rope-yarn, tied in a looped knot. The rough frock the woman wore had a heavy weave; the nap was worn at her knees, where she scrabbled in the earth doing the work of a peasant.

The sight of these people disturbed my brother and me. Who were they? Why were they here? We had rarely known strangers to travel to our door, we lived so far from anyone else.

We stood either side of our mother, clutching her. She seemed unmoved by these people as she motioned them into our home.

The Russian raised his voice and the man and woman moved quickly to the carriage, removing a heavy wooden kist and a large parcel made with a linen bedsheet, tied in a single knot.

I looked to Jurgis and saw his eyes following the packages as they were brought into our home.

The Russian spoke in a clear, clipped voice but his tone was not like that of our countrymen. "As you know," he said, "the Czar sees no reason for any one of his subjects to hold this type of property."

Our mother, sat motionless. She stared only to the floor, her eyes unmoving.

"And so," said the Russian, "we have installed a manager to oversee the Czar's interests."

My brother looked towards me for an explanation, but I had none.

"You will remain, the Empire has granted that," said the Russian, "but you can have no part in the running of the Czar's farm, save what the manager instructs you."

There was silence in the room, only the sifting of papers. "Do you understand?" said the Russian. He seemed perturbed. "Are you listening to me?"

Mother remained motionless and the Russian shook his head with frustration and then rose quickly to his feet.

"No one has the right to hold this type of property," the Russian said loudly. His broad face was fully red, except for the large whites of his eyes. "The Czar's farms are worked for the good of all his people."

He reached over to my mother and grabbed her by the jaw; turning her head, he bellowed in her ear, "The manager has our instructions. You will obey! You will assist!"

Within days of the Russian peasants taking over Father's farm I watched my brother crying as the flock was slaughtered.

Saule, the word for sun in our own language, was the name my brother gave to a lamb born to the farm. He treated the lamb like a puppy dog and as it grew Saule followed him around. The lamb trailed him like a pet or a young child, seeking him out each morning, long before any bird's song.

I knew it was painful to see the flock, which Jurgis cared so much for, turned over to the peasant named Kazimeras.

"I have not the bullets for a quick death," he told us, as he took first the ewes and pinned them down, to crack open their skulls with a hammer.

The animals fought. Kicking, they ran from the hammer and tried to escape the peasant's grasp, but he was a bear of a man and too strong for them to resist.

"No. No. No …" my brother cried out as each hammer blow came down upon the wailing flock.

The animals fell quickly and were piled high, the red and grey drools of their wounds seeping from their white gaping skulls.

"Come," said Kazimeras, his blank eyes bulging, his lower lip hanging like the belly above his rope-tied belt, "you can help drag the beasts away."

I took Jurgis by the arm and led him to where our father's once proud flock lay. "We must do as he says," I told him.

"But why?" sobbed Jurgis, "why must we?" He could not understand what he had seen. It had wounded us all deeply, but my poor Jurgis was felled by the sight which I wished I could have shielded him from.

"We must, Jurgis … we have no choice."

Mother and Kazimeras's wife, Ruta, lifted the carcasses by their hinds and loaded up the carts. Filled with the day's slaughter, the carts soon stood piled high before us, at the edge of our father's pastures.

When we were finished, the peasant sat down on his

heels and spoke: "Where are the men I was promised?" said Kazimeras. He looked all about, in every direction, his heavy lip drooping like a tucker bag. "Where are the men to remove the carts?"

We waited longer, but the men did not come to take the carts away. After a day the blood of our father's flock brought wolves and lynx from the forest. Black clouds of flies settled over the carts and maggots writhed in the gruesome decay that was once living flesh and blood. By week's end even the wool was rotten, worthless.

Kazimeras rested one hand upon his hip and swiped at flies with the other as he took in the scene. "We must dig a pit."

Every inch of the land was vital, we had nowhere to bury the beasts hereabouts. "Where?" I asked.

"Where we have space for such a vast pit – in the low pastures." Kazimeras strode towards the carts; his face became twisted as he neared the decay's stench, but he did not flinch from the task. He grasped the nearest handle firmly within his hands and then he hitched it high upon his shoulder.

As the cart's wheels turned my brother and I followed Kazimeras with our eyes; I knew he was headed for the best of my father's land. "But what will become of the pastures?" I called out.

"We shall see," said Kazimeras, "come, take up the carts."

For three days we dug in the low pastures. When we were finished digging, my father's land was the graveyard of his once proud flock. What was once pristine and green land was now riven and scarred, a place where black rooks fed upon its surface.

Though I stared and stared, I could little comprehend the change. "Nothing can graze here," I said.

"No," said Kazimeras. He crouched low and sifted the soil through his plump red fingers. "I will plant this land now … with potatoes."

Chapter Sixteen

A settler's hut in the island's west became our new home.

Rain ran down the walls in streams the colour of mustard that gathered on the earthen floor. Winter forced its way in through gaps between the planks, where beyond, flour sacks lined our cots. The door was held with wooden pegs, which blew out in the high winds that set the rusty hinges screeching.

"Myko, the door," called out Father.

I ran to force back the door; the bark roof was about to start its cracking, threatening to leave the four walls where they stood.

"Is it tight?" asked Father.

I pressed the door's bar; the pegs held firm. "Yes, it doesn't move an inch."

"Then come back to the warmth."

Mother knelt by the fire, rocking gently to and fro as though before a blessed altar, and spoke in our native words, "*Sacred Gabija*, forged, may you lay, kindled, may you shine."

I sat silently and watched her make a bed for the fire, delicately pouring ashes around its contours. Closely Mother arranged the cuts of wood in the homefire and then placed more neatly round its base.

As the fire began to crackle, flames leaped from the wood. Mother turned to look at me; I saw a heavy sagging beneath her eyes, but said nothing. Her mouth became a tight little knot holding in her words and thoughts. Her once elegant features now seemed pained to me.

I watched and when she spoke Mother addressed the fire as *Ungis*.

"Praise to you, *Ungis*," she said.

Mother placed a jug of clean water by the fire, "*Ungis,* may you have the water needed to cleanse yourself."

She sprinkled some salt into the flames and said, "*Sacred Gabija*, be satiated."

I saw the fire grow and the heat spread throughout the small room. Mother's face reddened before me and white pearls of moisture broke over her cheeks.

Her dark hair was soft as velvet; reflecting back the fire's glow, it glistened from root to tip. "*Sacred Gabija, our calmer, be still, be rapid. For ages and forever,*" said Mother, and then she stood and faced me, smiling. "Myko, you cannot speak, or look away even," she insisted.

I sat calmly before her, recording her words. My mother had become absorbed in these old country superstitions as never before.

"If a visitor is to appear at our doorway," she said, "his call must go unanswered – the fire cannot be extinguished this day."

I nodded as she formed her words.

"There can be no harsh talk in front of the fire this day," she continued, "the fire must not hear insults. It is not to be harmed. There will be no spitting in the fire, or kicking of the embers this day. Do you understand?"

I nodded before my mother once more, though I did not know why, my thoughts were coiled up like a bowline. I wished for one thing alone, to bring some peace to my mother's sicklike mind.

"All of these actions are sinful and inviting of punishment," said Mother, "either whilst alive, or after death."

Her words startled me and a long silence stretched out between us; yet her words seemed to hang in the air like loops of smoke.

"But how after death?" I said quietly.

The question made Mother flinch; her cold blue eyes froze on me. She knelt down and as the fire flickered behind her a long black shadow fell upon the wall.

"The dead live on, my boy," said Mother, as her eyes narrowed, "in the hearth of the fire dwell our ancestors. We must honour them always."

I did not know what to say, I felt as spooked as a horse which has just encountered a copperhead snake in its path. A sharp spasm of fear entered me, but I asked no more questions.

I had heard my mother talk many times of the old country ways. She talked of our traditions and the tales which were carried with them, but I knew now they kept a hold on her, which tightened by the day.

"Do you understand, Myko?" she said.

I knew I must accept my mother's ways with wonder. It was improper to press her for answers that this world did not have. "Yes, Mama," I said, "I understand."

My mother raised herself from the fireside and her long, loose gown dragged upon the dusty floor as she moved towards our eating table. She seemed to glide like a swan upon calm waters, her movements as seamless as if being drawn by a string.

As Mother raised her elbow the coffee-pot caught an arc of sunlight coming through the window and a million tiny dust specks were lit in the air. The grey liquid that she poured from the coffee-pot had a strong smell and it floated to the four walls and the roofbeams.

My mother passed a small tin cup to my father where he sat by the doorway, lacing-up his square-toed bluchers. "Do not go, Petras," she said.

My father said nothing, and my mother repeated her plea: "Do not go." Her voice was soft, but a quiver in its tone betrayed her emotions.

"I must," said Father.

"No, Petras, you cannot go." Mother dropped to her knees, locking her arms around Father's legs as tight as a ball of twine.

"I have seen your suffering in my dream."

"But I have our keep to earn." As he stood up my father coped easily with the strain of my mother's grasp. "Myko, my rifle," he said, motioning to the rack above my head.

"No, you cannot!"

Mother became frantic, she wailed out as if in terror. It was a pained and mournful cry. I had not heard such sounds within these walls before.

Mother threw herself on the ground in front of my father and grabbed tight around his legs, she lay atop his heavy bluchers, weeping. "Stay, stay with me," she called out.

Father raised her from the floor. "Stop, stop with this." He gathered her up in his arms and carried her to her crib, laying her down gently and stroking her brow. "Hush, hush," he said over and over again. But my mother did not calm any.

All colour left her face; my mother's pale lips held taught as soapy white deposits gathered in their corners and she began to shake all over in her crib, bobbing like a piece of driftwood on a choppy swell.

"Calm now, Daina," said Father, "you must be calm, I have to go now."

Father made to leave, reaching up for his rifle as he hurried for the door. "Attend to your mother, Myko," he called to me as he went.

I tried to comfort my mother some more, but I feared my words had little effect on her as she lay before me in her agony.

"It was just a dream," I said, "we all have unpleasant dreams, Mama. You have told me this yourself many times."

I watched her curl in her bunk as though afflicted by a harsh pain and then my mother turned over, bent like a hinge, and cried.

"My Myko you do not understand," she said, "I have seen

97

your father's death. A wife does not dream such things. How it must be true."

"No, Mother a dream is only a dream." I laid my hand on her head; stroking gently I tried to calm her, to take away her troubled thoughts.

My mother sat up and gripped tight on my arm. "My Myko, my darling boy." I felt an unusual strength in her grasp as she spoke. "I dreamt of the story of the *takmakas* … and your father was the traveller. The tigers became the wolves and … he died, that should not happen. It must not!"

"Mother, it will be all right." I did not know the story or understand how any mere tale disturbed her so cruelly.

"But, what of the *takmakas*?" Her words were whispered now, she was cautious, as if she did not want to tempt fate with her speech.

"I do not know anything about such things, Mother."

She blinked quickly before me, and then her eyes were wide and still. "I have not told you the tale of the *takmakas?*"

I shook my head at once, "No, Mother, you have not told me."

"Then of course you cannot understand, my son. How could you understand? I must tell you now," she said; her speech quickened, her tone was iron-rigid, "yes I must tell."

Mother ran her fingers through her long hair; as she did so I could see the thoughts gathering behind her widened eyes. "Once a traveller was riding along a road," she said, "in my dream he was your father. When the traveller came to a great forest there was a man stood outside. 'You better not ride in the forest', he told him, 'There are many wolves … you will be attacked if you go there'. But the traveller said, 'I have a musket'. 'What else have you got?' asked the man. 'I have a mighty sword'. 'And?' asked the man. 'I have, I have a *takmakas*', said the traveller."

98

"What is a *takmakas?*" I interrupted.

"Oh my Myko," said Mother, "the man did not know what it was either. It is a tobacco-crusher, but you see, the man did not know this because he was really a werewolf. Though he would often bewitch and ruin all the weapons that he knew of, he could do nothing with the *takmakas*."

I did not have my mother's deep attachment to such traditions but I took an interest in the tale. "So what became of the traveller?"

"After asking the questions, the man who was a werewolf walked on his way. And so the traveller rode into the forest, but after some time, a wolf blocked his path. The traveller tried to fire his musket, but nothing happened. He drew his sword, but the blade was blunt and did not make a scratch on the wolf. And then he drew his *takmakas* and struck blows on the wolf, hitting so hard that it was badly hurt. The wolf withdrew instantly, and the traveller continued on his way." My mother raked the air with her delicate fingers to signal the final curtain's descent upon her tale.

"That does not seem such a bad story, Mama."

"Ah, my Myko, but in my dream your father had no *takmakas*, and the wolf, remember, was a tiger!"

The telling seemed to calm my mother, so I listened some more, glad to be of comfort to her. She spoke of the old country longingly but the island, I could see, was a place of dread to her.

"The widow woman we took this hut from, her husband was once a tiger man," she said.

I knew the man had also been employed by the Van Diemen's Company, but I kept quiet, storing my thoughts away for myself only. "I know," I said.

"They let him go when he failed to catch any more tigers," said Mother. "They say, my Myko, he then turned his gun upon himself."

I did not want to see my mother upset any more. "Don't talk like this," I said, raising my voice higher.

"His widow told us there was no peace to be found in this homestead," said Mother, "she believed it to be cursed."

"Cursed? Mama, there are no curses here!" I grew defiant. I knew this kind of talk had already damaged my mother's way of thinking.

"The widow told me that the family which occupied the hut before her had awoken one morning to find their baby girl snatched from its crib." Mother's face became fixed, as if she were in a trance. I laid a hand upon her shoulder and tried to bring her back to me.

"No more talk, Mama."

"They found the child in one of the paddocks. Its throat had been gnawed into shreds."

"*Mama, stop.*" My words were useless.

"The child's heart and liver had been eaten, its body was a ghostly shade of grey where she lay upon the morning's dew."

"Mama, no." I wished to hear no more. I raised a hand to her mouth to try and silence her, but it was knocked away. My mother did not respond to my comforting.

"The widow blamed the island's tigers, which were numerous then, but none were ever captured. There were only the island's devils, which made a mighty protest when the child was taken from them."

I rose to my feet. "Mama, I have not known of any tiger to attack a man," I told her. My knees were shaking as I spoke. "I don't believe all the tales … they are peaceful creatures, they have more to fear from us than we do from them."

My mother motioned me to sit once more; she spoke slowly now. "Myko, I know your father's trade is an unholy one."

Her words calmed me, and I felt the fists I held loosen.

"I know God in his heaven must find ways to punish such doings."

My father had strayed far from the old ways. It was true he took the side of much that was against the old beliefs.

"We do not need to store up such things now, Mama," I said, "we are no longer in the Sakiai."

Suddenly my mother stood to face me; her eyes cut hollows in me that led clear to my soul. "Do you think because we are not in the Sakiai, God will not see us?" Her tone was changed, she sounded deeply serious, as if moved close to rage. "Do not be foolish, Myko! Do not be foolish! Sin is sin, wherever the stone is cast ... the man who has thrown it must face his actions."

Chapter Seventeen

My mother's fears came to nothing; the tigers which clung to the island's far reaches had grown ever scarcer, and Father returned from his hunt unscathed.

As soon as he appeared, a pack of boys trailed him along the road from the station. "Have you a tiger, sir?" called a boy.

My father kept his steady gaze facing front as a young boy ran before him and waved his arms to rouse my father. "Tiger man! Tiger man!" he roared out.

Father's horse dropped its neck sharply, flashing a long stretch of mane behind it. "Step aside," called Father, "get out of my way!"

The pack of boys let out wheezy laughs as they followed at my father's back. They pulled at each other and lolled from side to side in their merriment as they kept inside father's tracks.

Upon the hillside, where I watched the scene played below, I turned to Tilly. She sat atop a five-bar fence, her wheaten hair-bunches blowing in the breeze.

"He won't be pleased," I said.

"Why?"

"There's no tiger … he won't be pleased."

Tilly jumped down from the fence. "Maybe he's already taken his haul to Hobart."

"No. He wouldn't do that, Tilly."

"Why not? That's where they pay the bounty, doesn't he want the bounty?"

I let out a sigh. My father moved beyond our view of the track below.

"Those trees over there … look Tilly," I pointed to the broad leatherwoods that stood tall by the paddocks, taking the sun's full glare.

"What about them?" said Tilly.

"When he has a tiger, my father pegs the skin out for drying on those trees. We can see the trees from our hut, he likes to watch people pass by and look at them."

Tilly turned first to the leatherwoods and then towards my family's crude split-paling hut. Gentle creases appeared on her brow as she tracked the distance between the two, and then she spoke. "He will not be pleased," she said.

I moved towards the fence and sat on the dry patchy grass, resting my back on the holding-post. Tilly followed and sat at my side. "Sometimes, when my father comes home from catching fish, he can be spiteful ... if he's no fish."

I smiled and Tilly turned on her knees to face me. "Will he be really mad?"

I had no time to answer her. Below us, past the paddock's fringe, my father called for me. I could hear his voice roaring above the treetops, "Myko, Myko."

I jumped to my feet. "I have to go now, Tilly," I said and I left her kneeling in the dry grass as I made for home.

On the low foothills and green stretches that bordered the plains the grass tufts thinned as I ran. Bracken and spiky-leafed pandani scratched my shins and tugged at my steps.

When I reached below the hill I turned back to look for Tilly, but she was gone.

"Myko, Myko," called out my father again. I knew he had seen me running. He was eager to have me home and would not see me dally any.

I pressed harder into the final stretch of track that led to our hut. Where my father stood, he clutched his hands tight behind his back. As I neared him I saw he held a stock whip which trailed him like a serpent's tail.

"Where have you been?" Father roared out as I came into the yard.

I turned to the hill, "There, only on the hill."

"Playing? Wasting your time, no doubt."

I shook my head, and then I looked around the yard. I knew my duties and I had not neglected them. "Father …"

"Be quiet," he interrupted. "Here, take this."

I took the stock whip from his hand.

"I must go to the station at Woolnorth," said Father, "you will have to attend the beasts."

I felt the stock whip's handle in my hand; it was smooth to the touch. "Yes, Father," I said, "but why are you going to the station?"

"What does it matter?" he snapped.

I lowered my head. I knew my words were an irritation to him; my father was sorely vexed.

"Just look after the beasts," he said, "can you manage that?"

"Yes."

"Then good. This is a busy time for the station. The dipping is soon to begin, all hands will be pressed into duty and I need to know you can handle things here."

As my father returned to his mount I watched my mother hand him a tucker bag, and wave to him. On his way Father pointed to the pasturelands and instructed I begin my duties.

I carried the stock whip by my side as I rounded the most errant of the flock. They were a boisterous longwool breed and regarded every fence as a challenge. It seemed no height of paling prevented their forays. Their antics kept me busy for some long hours.

The cloud-burdened sky turned bottle-green in the darkening day and the air, crisp and cool, carried the salty wash of the sea. The sleeping trees by the trackside seemed mournful figures as I trailed the flock through the slatted daylight that was turning fast to night.

As a kookaburra gave out its last laughing cry of the day the sky seemed to hold the stars prisoner. The wind revived itself and of a sudden I sensed a disturbance deep within the bush.

The grass grew heavy on the flats, save where it was trampled by the rat-runs, and made my work harder going in the growing darkness. The animals began to behave in a peculiar fashion, timid, and refused to move distances of more than a few feet from cover.

The wallabies became frantic, struggling with the slightest movement, which sent them scurrying, terrified, for shelter. I watched an echidna roll itself into a ball so tight that, were it not for the spikes upon its back, it could have been a large chestnut stone.

The wombats, increasing their ungainly steps, scurried beneath the gorse towards their hides. And the brush possum, like the bandicoot, climbed higher and higher in the trees until I could hardly see them. They fled out of sight, so far above me only the faintest shimmerings were visible under the moon's clear light.

I grew uneasy and unfurled Father's stock whip at my side then, in an instant, a strange sight greeted me. A wallaby came bounding from the scrub – dread marked the poor beast. It clearly feared for its life.

The wallaby appeared large for its type and a strong bound took it far from me after only a few seconds in my sight.

What is it running from? I wondered. What could put the animal in such fear?

I had no thoughts to intervene. But I saw that a stock whip offered no threat to the pursuer in this chase. I took the only option I had and sought cover in the branches of a stringy barked eucalypt.

I climbed high in the tree and the bare branches put the

ground below me in clear sight. As I picked out the wallaby running its circle, the moon lit the wide arc of the creature's leap; I knew it was fear that made it act this way.

My shoulders became heavy as they supported my weight in the tree's branches. I panted like a horse as my heart beat madly beneath my shirt. Then, suddenly, I felt the rhythmical throb in my chest begin to subside, as my gaze grabbed the sight before me.

A large bull tiger, his coat clear and his back strong, passed beneath me. If he sensed me, he was not disturbed. His nose was latched firmly upon the trail of the wallaby; he seemed utterly occupied with his hunt.

The tiger's tail pointed straight out, extended from his back, where the black stripes dashed across his rump. His gait stretched strongly. Unlike the leaping speed of a dog, the tiger moved like a feline, but bolder, more consistent. His deep chest and short legs made for the carriage of a more hardened hunter, equipped with the most basic of tools.

The tiger chased persistently, following fast upon the wallaby, tracing the arc of its circle, but never quite gathering the pace to bring it to ground.

Did the tiger plan to run it down with exhaustion? Did he accept these final laps as a prelude to the kill?

The tiger looked calm and familiar with his hunt. I knew I was watching an exacting ritual, something which had been replayed over thousands of years. But I did not see the tiger as cruel; his actions came as naturally as the wallaby's. I thought the tiger would strike at the wallaby, run it to the point of exhaustion and attack, but he did not.

The tiger broke free of the chase and let the wallaby begin its final tired revolution. As it did so, the tiger cut a line across the wallaby's bounding pathway.

The line of the tiger's run, and his timing, brought the

wallaby to ground. The kill was quick, the tiger's jaws clasping fully round the wallaby's neck, releasing it from the worries of this world in an instant.

As I watched the tiger feed, his murky-brown eyes shone beneath the uniform sky. He fed quickly, taking his nourishment quietly and without ceremony.

To see this sight I felt blessed, and then, my heart suddenly quickened, as the tiger's mate came into view.

The pair fed quickly, ripping open the wallaby's ribcage and devouring their prey heartily. How rare the tigers had become, to see two together, practising a kill, was something I knew I must hold dearly forever.

Few could have seen such a sight as this, but as I watched I was gripped by sinister thoughts. The tigers below me were on land my father held for the Van Diemen's Company. When he returned from the dipping, his dogs would seek them out.

My head became dizzy. Where I held myself in the tree I felt bound to fall as panic washed over me. I knew, as fine and strong as these tigers were, they were no match for my father's bullets.

"Go! Go from here!" I roared.

The tigers raised their heads to where I held on to the tree's branches. I shook the branches as hard as I could to scare them and summoned every unearthly cry that I could raise from within me.

"Go! Go from here!"

In less time than it had taken the tigers to appear, they fled my sight. I prayed I would never see them again.

Chapter Eighteen

As I woke early in our crude split-paling hut and rubbed at my tired eyes, my mother trod meekly around me. She took steps towards the fire where she began to boil a billycan, keeping quiet, I believed, so as not to wake my father.

"I will heat some cuts of bread," said Mother, "you may have an egg this morning, Myko, one of our very own eggs; there is no brightness like the yellow of a farm lain egg."

As my eyes found their focus, I looked around and saw that my father's bunk was empty.

"Where is Father?"

My mother seemed confused by the question. "He is at the station," she said.

For a moment my heart trembled beneath my nightshirt, and then I remembered; "Of course, the dipping," I said.

Mother stepped back from the fireside. She rubbed her hands upon her apron as she walked towards me. "Are you all right, Myko?"

"Yes, I am fine," I blurted, "I am fine, Mama."

She looked at me with caution in her eyes. The moment between us seemed to last for a long time, but then it passed and she returned to the fireside to prepare our food.

"You got back very late last night, Myko," she said, "you must still be tired."

"I'm all right. I have little to do today, Mama," I said, "I have only to go to Woolnorth, to the Three Strides Run, carting sackloads of flour to the bakers and share-farmers."

My father had kept my chores light, for at the dipping time all hands were put to use to make sure the station continued to run as smoothly as it always did.

"Still, you shall need your strength, Myko," said Mother.

"Here, eat up."

My mother placed some bread on my plate and returned to the fireside where she sat down and pulled her dark shawl around her bony shoulders. Where she sat, with her arms folded tightly across her chest, it was impossible to imagine that the fire's warmth could penetrate her cold grey frame.

"Will you not eat some with me, Mama?"

My mother did not answer me; did she hear me? Had she the strength for any more words? I watched her weakly stoke the red embers in the grate and then she lodged the last piece of hewn blue gum from the woodpile on top of the flames. Sparks flew up and hung momentarily in the air before turning to ashes and floating up into the chimney breast.

I was concerned by the sight before me. I had meant to chop wood for the homefire a day ago, but time slipped away from me. I was too taken up with other things. "Mama," I called out, "I shall cut some wood for you before I leave."

"It is all right, I can use an axe," she said weakly.

I could think of no worse task to set the frail figure slumped before me. "No, I will do it."

My mind returned to what had occupied me the day before. I recalled the events clearly, they appeared fresh to me, and I knew at once I must run the tigers from the station. If my father or the settlers found them, they would not survive.

My mother caught me raising my eyes aloft. I felt my brows knit and knew that I could not hide my thoughts and fears for the tigers from her.

My mother leaned forward in her chair; her shawl dipped below the line of her shoulders. "What is it, Myko?"

Quickly, I returned her gaze, "I don't know what you mean." At once I knew my words sounded unconvincing.

My mother stood up and walked soft-footed towards me. At my side she placed her cold hand on my cheek. She smiled sweetly as she spoke to me. "Myko, oh my Myko, I have seen your eyes wander … you cannot keep such things from your mother."

My speech became trapped within my throat for an instant. I lowered my mother's hand from my face and turned away from her. "No, I don't think so. Perhaps I am tired, like you say."

I panicked. I felt my breath grow heavy. As soon as I spoke my words became snatched, too loud to cover my fears, "I had very little sleep … I must be used to more."

My mother smiled once again. "Perhaps that is it."

I knew she did not believe me, but I felt relief that she pried no further. I saw her eyelids become heavy and her cheeks draw in as she returned to her chair at the fireside. I do not believe she had the strength to draw her suspicions from me.

I did not want to stay where I might betray myself any more, and I stood up to leave; "I will go and cut the wood for you now."

My mother's eyes did not move. As I walked to the door, she sat as motionless as if restrained by invisible hands. I wondered what thoughts now turned inside her head, but I dared not ask.

Outside the hut a dew had settled upon the paddocks and a cool breeze carried the scent of eucalyptus from the woodland beyond the coastal heath. I saw the acacia blossoms spreading, dense and aromatic, throughout the spiny wattle.

In the open my fears fell on the tigers I witnessed at hunt the night before, but I could not help but worry about my mother.

I collected branches which had fallen from the blue gums. They felt heavy and I had to heft high the axe to split their tough contours. I thundered through the firewood; the handle of the axe felt smooth and sure, familiar to my hands.

Soon I breathed heavily, my shirt turned damp with sweat. The work took me from my gloom and I did not want to stop, but as the woodpile filled, the six taut wires of its sides strained tightly.

I laid down the axe; as I did so I noticed the hut's door swinging noisily in the open air. Its hinges screeched like galahs and its latch worried at the jamb. At once I wondered why my mother left the door to blow in the wind and I strode clump-footed to the hut's entrance.

I did not know what to expect – had my mother left? Had she injured herself in some way and found herself unable to move? As I walked through the door my eyes seized a sight which struck me as hard as an iron fist.

My mother sat where I had left her, stock still, crumpled as an old handkerchief. I saw she held many miseries, which were stored deep within herself. She seemed to be stooped over a dark vault, for which she alone held the key. Had she shared her anguish with anyone? Did my father know of it?

"Mama," I said softly, but she did not respond.

Mother suffered, she had tried to keep strong, but I understood now that she possessed no strength for further trials.

I left her where she sat, and returned to the yard.

I caught sight of a dusky robin which settled on a stump beyond the woodpile. I watched it jump between the split logs, hoping to uncover a louse. For some minutes I stared at the small bird's efforts; it did not seem to tire.

"Are you done, my Myko?" said Mother. I was startled to see she had raised herself and followed me back out to the yard.

"I will cut some more wood for the fire," I said.

"No, you must go now."

I picked up the axe and raised it above me. "Just a few more, it may get cold later in the day."

I let fly with the heavy blade; its head lunged into the gum branch and was buried to its hilt. I knew my stores of anger could sustain me, my father had his labours; but what about my mother?

She faced her torment alone, with no one to turn to. I longed for her to reach out to me, but her grasp never came. As I glanced upon her where she stood before the acacia blossoms, I knew there never would be any such call from her.

"That is enough, Myko. Go now, I can manage fine on my own."

I lowered the axe and turned from her.

I cared deeply for my mother but I now feared the cast of her mind had grown as fragile as frost upon a meadow.

Chapter Nineteen

I travelled to Woolnorth and, though lost in duty, my mind wandered. At the brow of the settlement's hill I gazed across the landscape, searching for my tiger. I knew the tigers ranged over many miles when they took to the coastal runs, but I did not see any sign of them.

The sun shone down on the sea and pulled shivering yellow lines high above where the sea birds circled into the clouds. The water ran deep and green where it met the shore and then carried itself twinkling over sands and rock pools.

I heard the calls of the honeyeaters and knew they kept at work, stripping the dry bark from the eucalypts and fetching out the insects beneath. I heard the currawongs too and looked to see their black wings spread and soaring above the foothill slopes.

I set my eyes upon the full view of the station. I saw the valleys and canopies, the tracks and sandy banks and the hillsides running deep and green, beaten hard by the heavy treading of the flocks. But I saw no tiger.

I knew I should not see my tiger during the daylight. The wise beast rested during the day, so he could hunt under the cover of darkness. But in these settled lands I still worried – my tiger might be disturbed. As if in tune to the notion my eye suddenly jerked upon a flash of fawn coat. It made my heart quicken. When I narrowed my gaze to the blurred form, however, I saw only a pack dog, running as aimlessly and wildly as all pack dogs do.

I gazed for hours, looking far and wide for the tigers, but soon the day neared its end and the sun settled low on the horizon like the last light of a sinking ship.

The water turned to a deep and dark shade of purple and

the clouds came down to make a long grey line as ragged as a saw's teeth above the swell.

I followed the hum of endeavour which came from the station where all hands had turned towards the dipping. The great flocks required much attention and hardly a boy or man was left who had not rolled up his sleeves and stepped into gumboots to play a part, however small or flighty.

A lantern lolled out of the distance and came swaying towards me. I saw Tilly smiling as she came into sight, grasping tightly on the lantern's handle. "Myko, Myko," she called out.

I returned her smile and waved. At once I longed to tell her about the tigers I had seen, but I knew my secret must be kept hidden from everyone, even Tilly.

"They won't let me help with the dipping."

"Why?" I asked her.

"Because I'm a girl … it is man's work they said." Tilly blew up her cheeks and raised her arms up above her head, showing her muscles like we had seen the strongmen do in picture books. I laughed out loud. When she heard me laughing Tilly could not hold in her breath, she burst open her mouth and her cheeks closed like bellows as she laughed with me.

"Where have you been?" said Tilly. As we walked in the fading light men paced back and forth, their heads bowed in concentration. It was like watching a circus's arrival, the whole troupe mustered to raise the top before light failed and the footfall of the night's customers came.

"I have been minding my father's flock."

"So they won't let you near the dipping, either." Tilly pointed to the men at the dipping well. "It's a fussy business … the sheep don't like it, look."

A hundred sheep passed into the well, poked and prodded on the points of broom handles. I saw not one that welcomed the process. We watched as they emerged, wet and wounded from the experience, their sense of the fight lost to them once again.

"They take it so seriously." Tilly swung the lantern from side to side, making rings of light in the air before us.

"They have no time for capers," I said, "a drowned sheep costs the station dearly, says my father."

We watched together as some boys we knew to be fools led away the wet and shaken animals from their chaos. Tilly let out a long, slow breath. I could tell the dipping time made her restless. As I looked at her I saw her eyes rolling up to the sky and I longed again to share my tiger sighting with her, but I knew it must remain my secret.

"This will go on for days," said Tilly, "days and days …"

I knew that with the dipping underway my tiger had chosen his time well. Had he shown in the quieter months, he might not have survived a day. I was glad to see the station given over to such toil and fervour.

"It's the busiest time of the year, the dipping," I said, "my father says when the work is done there will be time to play."

"Fiddles in the barn, and dancing."

"Yes, when they're finished."

A pair of roo dogs began to bark beyond the dipping well. As I watched the dogs they seemed to be truly disturbed, but no one paid them any attention. The noise unsettled me, however, and I wondered, had they caught a tiger scent.

"I have to go, Tilly."

"But, why?"

"I just have to go," I said, breaking into a run.

"Myko …"

"I have to go," I shouted, "I have to."

At another time there may have been hunts raised, snares set and trappings mustered, but a roo dog's barking gathered little attention with the station men engaged in such a solemn

115

duty. But still they unsettled me as I ran for home.

As I went I heard the song of the reed warblers and knew day's end fast approached. They sang from the tops of reed spikes, announcing their presence and territorial rights to all, but I could not see any of these wary birds.

On the road I took up a number of Huon pines from a hawker. He collected the slim tree shanks in the southern rainforests where the loggers that claimed the larger pines left them behind.

The wood smelled sweetly and felt hard to the touch as I dragged my pines by a firm hemp rope, secured with a reef knot, along the dry track to home.

The night's dusk came creeping down from the hills and the ragged mountains beyond. I heard the curlews stirring by their roosting sites in the salt marshes. They foraged in the sandy spits and rocky outcrops for ghost shrimps and creeper crabs. Where I watched them their down-curving bills and mottled plumage were unmistakable, as they waded in the eelgrass beds, waving their open bills to detect their prey.

I cut a path through the sedge and bracken to home. At the edge of the cleared land, by the stone wall, a cloud of blowflies rose to greet me. Chooks came running through the yard and by the hut's side I saw weeds beginning to creep.

Inside, my mother sat like a beaten dog, barely lifting her head to greet me as I went to her side at the table.

"Mama," I said, lowering on my heels to face her. She seemed to be deep in concentration, her mind wandering far away.

"Ah, Myko, you are home." My mother rose from her chair and directed me to sit where Father always served us at the table.

"But, this is Father's place," I said.

"Sit. Sit, Myko."

116

In the Sakiai we observed strict order at mealtime. Father sat at the table's end and I, being his eldest son, sat to his right. My brother then sat beside me, and my mother sat opposite Father. Our daily bread stayed on the table's most honourable position, before Father, and our eating always began with his cutting of the bread.

"Here, have the bread, Myko."

"But, Mama … this is Father's duty." I recalled how he sliced and passed the bread with great respect, the first piece, a corner, always going to myself and carrying the wish that my firstborn be a son.

"Myko, your father is not here."

It did not feel right. I protested: "He is only at the station. He will be back when the dipping is over."

"Myko, your Father is not here now. Do as I tell you."

I sliced into the bread and offered it as I had seen my father do many times before. Mother took a piece of bread and placed it respectfully before her. When this was done, I placed the bread facing the corner of the room. I knew we must never put the bread upside down, but I did not know why.

"Mother, why must we never turn over the bread?" Immediately I looked away, I had broken the table's peace and displeased my mother.

Her milky eyes took me in. "Because," she said calmly, "it brings death to the family."

I wanted to leave the table and go to the flock and Father's snare lines at once. I lowered my head and wished I had thought to keep my words to myself. I stared at the curd cheese, the sausages and the round edible mushrooms collected from the forest groves, which my mother still called, *grybai*.

"I am worried about you Myko … what is it?"

As I shook my head, I saw her fingernails were bitten low to the quick, the skin around them cracked and broken.

"Nothing, there is nothing wrong."

"I did not ask what is wrong. I asked only to know what it is that occupies you."

I fought a need to pause. "It is nothing, Mama." I rushed out the words and did little to convince my mother she had nothing to fear.

"Well, then is there something wrong after all?"

I wanted to end our talk, "No, Mama. I am fine." I raised myself from the table, "I have my duties, Mama." I held fire within me hot as any furnace coke for what I must do.

Mother watched me as I collected my father's stock whip and rolled it in my hands. "Be careful," she said, "you must take care."

My mind hardened. "I have only the flock to check." I knew this was a lie, but I knew also I must protect my mother from further troubles.

"Myko, you are my son. I know when you must take care."

"Yes, Mama, I will take care."

I left her alone, I feared, to worry some more.

Chapter Twenty

After the soldiers took Father from us, our life in the Sakiai changed completely.

In our own home, where we once had been so happy, where Mother and Father read us the old stories by the fire, taught us our prayers and watched us at play with our toys, we found we now had masters to answer to.

"They are not like our people … they are our conquerors and enslavers," Mother said to me.

I knew Kazimeras and Ruta came to us from Russia and they could not be trusted. Any wrong word or deed from us was likely to be reported back to the Russians, Mother told me.

Kazimeras sat in Father's chair. He broke the bread first, like Father. Our mother could not watch him, but Ruta took great pride in her husband's passing of the bread to us all. She smiled, her peasant's face beamed and her great round cheeks shone like bright red apples before us.

Kazimeras grinned back, showing his teeth to be rotten in his head; like little greying fossils these stumps stood proud of their black gums. How I longed to hammer them down, flatten them from our sight, just as he had done with Father's flock.

"Myko, eat your bread," my mother told me. But I could not, I felt my temper stretched as tightly as a tarpaulin.

"I won't eat this bread with them!" I roared, as I ran from the table.

I could not watch them in our home, or be near them anymore. My mother followed at my heels, I heard her cries trail quickly behind me, "*Myko, Myko*," she called out to me, "what is the matter?"

I rushed up the stairs, and howled: "There!" I pointed to

our supper table and let out a roar, "It is not their home ... it is ours!"

My mother continued to move quickly towards me; as she did so she snatched a glance at Kazimeras and Ruta where they sat watching.

"Myko, come here," called my mother. Her hands were outstretched as she latched onto my ankles and brought me down.

"No. No. No." I lashed out, trying to free myself from her grasp.

Where I fell upon the stairs Mother swept me towards her, clasping me tightly in her arms, and ran towards her room. As we went I felt her place a hand over my mouth. All the while I watched her taking little furtive glances through the balustrades towards Kazimeras and Ruta, who stared back with their mouths wide in disbelief.

"That is enough now, Myko. You must be quiet." Mother's face was held tightly, her brows pinched on her eyes, as she lowered me down and closed fast the door of her room.

"Can't you see that it must be this way, Myko?" my mother scolded me. She trembled as she spoke. Her hands still held me tightly but their movement did not subside.

"It must be this way, Myko," said Mother loudly as she shook me to my senses, "it must be this way ... can't you understand that?"

I knew not to question her further. I sensed the fear my mother held within herself.

By New Year's Eve our household grew stable enough to come together with the people of the village. Though I still carried anger sharp as a blade, I knew to keep it hidden.

Straw fires burned and bells rang out to celebrate the New Year. Kazimeras and Ruta drank barley wine and broke bread with the villagers. A brother of Ruta's appeared, too, and spoke of witchings and other tall tales.

"Daina, Daina ..." Ruta called out my mother's name, "Daina, come, come with us indoors, we have something to show you."

Ruta's eyes sparkled like tiny stars; her breath became heavy as she ran to gather up my mother in her arms and rush her from us.

"Come on, Jurgis," I told my brother, "we must follow." We crept behind Mother, uneasy to let her out of our sight.

As we walked we heard much talk of the proper traditions we must perform at this time. People spoke of what the coming year might bring.

"Will the year be lucky or unlucky?" a man called to my mother.

She smiled, but gave no reply to the man.

"Will there be a good or a bad harvest, Daina?" called out another, removing his hat and bowing before her.

"Will our oppressors be merciful or unjust?" said yet another.

My mother clutched at her coat collars and moved delicately among the crowd, smiling as she went. My brother and I trailed her like little attendants to a mighty queen. We had never seen so many people who wished to talk to our mother.

"Were there to be a blizzard," said Ruta's brother, Pranciskis, "it would auger well for the crops."

As he followed us indoors we saw that Pranciskis was lame; the heavy boot on his weak limb scraped loudly on the floor.

"And magpies," he said, "we must pray for magpies, many, many magpies covering the garden when we wake, for that will bring us many new and welcome additions to our family."

"Oh, Ruta," said my mother. I knew she did not want to think of such things.

"No, no, this is a special time," said Ruta, "the only time, just once a year, when we can speak with such certainty."

I sensed that Ruta, like all the peasants, felt her country's old traditions deeply.

My brother and I stood still at our mother's side, as still and as calm as the few great trees that rested with their branches frozen by winter's chills upon Father's land.

We glanced up at our mother to check for changes in her face, but none came. It seemed as if my mother felt too afraid to allow any hint of emotion to seep out, lest it betray her, and my brother and me as well.

"Now," said Ruta, "watch what I do."

She placed a glass filled with water by the mirror on the wall.

"This is my mother's," said Ruta holding up a wedding ring, "she is dead," she added, nodding quickly.

Ruta dropped the wedding ring into the glass of water and then put her plump fingers around its base as she began to stir the water with two long white stork feathers.

"You see, you must look," she called to my mother, "look, look in there at the ring, do you see it?"

Mother peered into the glass. As she stretched her long white neck the lace collar of the crimson dress she wore showed beneath her coat. I knew this dress came in a present from my father, I remembered the joy on my mother's face when he brought it home to her. My mother had not worn the dress since my father was taken from us.

"Well, well, do you see?" said Ruta.

Mother was silent. Her eyes moved between Ruta and the glass as though she sought guidance.

"Is there a face?"

My mother shook her head and gathered her coat's collar tightly around her neck. The crimson dress was hidden beneath.

"Look, there must be a face. Keep looking, there must be a face."

My mother continued to stare into the glass. The stork feathers swirled faster and faster as Ruta bit down on the tip of her plum-coloured tongue.

"What face?" said Jurgis.

"*Shush*," I told him. I was engrossed in the scene playing out before us.

"What face, Myko? What face does she see?" pried Jurgis, but I waved off his pestering.

Soon Ruta's plump hand grew tired and she lowered the glass. It clunked loudly on the hardwood and the mirror on the wall swayed where it hung. "Oh, it is all a waste! You have not done it properly, Daina!" she called out.

My mother looked confused; I do not think she knew what Ruta expected of her.

Mother narrowed her eyes; they took the shape of little almonds. "What was I supposed to see, Ruta?" my mother said. Her voice was low and calm as she spoke to our masters.

"To see," snapped Ruta, "why, the face of your new husband!"

Mother's eyes widened and they started to bulge at their whites, I thought their black centres would be forced out and fly like tiny arrows into Ruta.

"I have a husband," said my mother. Her voice was louder now; it fell as weighty as lead.

Ruta swiped away the glass with the back of her hand and, at once, it smashed into pieces on the floor. The crashing noise brought a loud gasp from the room.

My brother and I fell paralysed where we stood. We did not know what to expect as we watched the water drip from the table's edge and the stork feathers float gently to the floor, like the snow falling outside the window.

"I have a husband," said my mother once more; her voice held less strength when she said it the second time. Mother looked overcome by her emotions.

"Now, now," said Ruta. Her demeanour changed quickly, she seemed calmer as she approached and placed her plump hands on Mother's delicate shoulders. I saw a tremble pass through my mother at Ruta's touch.

"Now, now," said Ruta again, "you must accept he is gone. It is time for you to move on, Daina … it is time for you to take a new husband."

My mother fell silent. She seemed a great distance from us all, close enough to touch, but as unreachable as the marrow of our bones.

Ruta's plump hands forced Mother into a chair. Where she sat she stared at the floor. My brother and I went to her side and I placed my arm around her trembling shoulders, but I felt I was of little comfort to her.

"I have a husband," said Mother, "I do … don't I?"

My mother looked towards me but I did not get to answer as Ruta lunged at me and rushed Jurgis and me outside, where the snow fell heavily on the ground. "Go … go and find dry tree branches for everyone," said Ruta.

I wanted to be indoors with my mother. "Why? What for?" I asked.

"To place in the fallen snow, of course," said Ruta, her voice suddenly lively. I knew it as the voice adults adopted to distract children, to coax them quickly to their will, "In the morning we shall check the branches and those whose are still standing up will have a prosperous New Year."

I looked to see my mother through the window, as Ruta quickly ushered us out of doors. "Go, go now," said Ruta, shooing us with her arms, her cheeks flushed red as the sun in the evening's sky.

I looked once more beyond Ruta to my mother. Her arms had fallen flat to her sides, her coat flapped open and it revealed the dress my father had given her.

At my mother's side I spied Pranciskis, leaning over her, his crooked leg hanging behind him like a cruel shadow.

"When we check in the morning, what if the branch is fallen over?" said Jurgis.

"Well, then," said Ruta, "then there will be a death before the next new year.

Chapter Twenty-One

I dragged my haul of Huon pines to the woodpile and let the axe fly into their hard shanks. They were as straight as a tall ship's mast and solid as stone within.

I could heft an axe from dusk until dawn and gain no more discomfort than a few calluses upon my hands, and I tore through the trees like a demon. With each blow I tried to spend the angry energy that ran through me like a poison. My mind held only one thought: How will I hide my tiger?

Even if I snared or trapped him, what possible chance did I have of capturing his mate as well? I knew the tiger population had grown scarce and I might have encountered one of the last pairs on the island. My actions must be swift.

"What are you thinking about, Myko?" I turned to see Tilly sitting on the yard's stone wall, her bare feet swinging before her.

I said nothing and returned to the pines, taking up the axe again.

"It's tigers!"

"*What?*"

"You are thinking of tigers," she jumped down from the wall and walked towards the woodpile, swaying her arms as she went, "I can tell."

I put down the axe, "How?"

"Because, Myko … it is all you think about."

I knew I had watched my father at a spree of killing and done nothing to halt it; I wondered, was my guilt as girded as his? Could Tilly see it?

"It's not true," I tried to cover my feelings, "I was thinking of something else."

Tilly stuck out her neck, her head jutted into my face,

"What?"

"Nothing that would interest you."

"Tell me."

"*No.*"

She danced around me, pulling at my shirttails as I tried to avoid her gaze. "Tell me. Tell me. Tell me," she sang.

"All right," I said, "just stop, and I'll tell."

Tilly stood before me; she closed her lips tightly and held her hands behind her back.

"I was thinking about my old home."

"What about it?"

"I was thinking how different it was to here on the island."

Tilly tilted her head to the side, "You don't like it here, do you?"

"I didn't say that I didn't like it. I was just thinking of my old home."

I went to sit down on the woodpile. Tilly followed and sat at my side. "Tell me something about your old home."

"Tell you what?"

"Just something about it … something that happened."

I could think of nothing to tell her. "Like what"

"I don't know, just something." I heard impatience creeping in Tilly's voice.

I picked up a small pebble and threw it into the air; it carried over the yard and came down on the road. "I will tell you a strange thing that happened once."

Tilly turned around and brought her head down to rest upon the back of her clasped hands. "Tell me then, tell me."

"Once, when I was travelling home with my father, I saw a beggar man."

Tilly interrupted, "What did he look like?"

"He was unwashed. His elbows and knees poked through his clothes and he was slumped in the road."

"What happened when you saw him?"

"My father called him over. 'Come here, my friend,' he said. And then he unwrapped some rye bread and held it out to the beggar man."

"Did he take it?"

"At first I was scared to look as he came to us, but then I saw him raise his thin arm. It looked like a twig."

Tilly shifted her head, "Did he take the bread?"

"He took the bread. I looked into his face, but the beggar man's eyes were closed tight."

"He closed his eyes?"

"Yes."

"Why?"

"I don't know," I said. I knew my story confused Tilly. "When I asked my father why he gave the beggar man our bread, he said, 'We must always help those who need our help'."

Tilly stood up and brushed down her long trousers. "That is a strange story, Myko."

"I have been thinking about it a lot lately." I rose to my feet. "Tilly, I have to go, I have the flocks to see to."

I picked up my lantern and tucker bag and turned toward the track for the coastal runs to check on Father's flock.

Tilly waved to me as I went.

My eyes were slitted against the wind as I crossed a low hillock. I saw the moon shining on the great stretch of sea beyond the coast. Little ripples broke on the black surface and gathered in greater rolls to lash the crags further inland.

I heard scarcely any noise, save the murmurings of the sea – its suck and wash – and the crackling of crushed twigs and bark beneath my steps.

As I came upon the sheep I found them quiet in their pens as they clung together like cobwebs in the dark. A few stirrings and bleatings broke out here and there, but the flock remained secure. I was pleased by this; I had much to occupy me and I knew the flock would suffer if they needed my attentions.

I set out on the less travelled tracks, in search of my tiger.

I moved towards the wild unsettled country that stuck like a solid wedge at the bourne of the station's cleared land. I had no plan, save an unformed desire to warn my tiger to leave this unsafe trail.

My father would return soon. His duties would be light in the coming days whilst he regained his strength following the dipping, but his dogs would be active. They were taught to fasten upon a tiger scent and would begin to hunt as soon as they arrived.

As I searched for my tiger I knew he was no nearer sanctuary than when I first laid eyes on him. I had dwelled on the plight of my tiger for days and my search brought me no rest from the panic I felt.

My heart hardened and my mind grew as sharp as the spine tipped branchlets of the bitter pea's prickly shrub: my course was set, I would do all I could to save my tiger.

My senses became heightened as I wandered through the ragged and twisted strands of tanglefoot which crossed my path. The lantern lit the way beyond me and shone further into the dense wood, but I saw nothing there except a single set of owl eyes which caught me unawares upon a low branch. The owl let out a flat hoot and I removed the lantern's glare quickly.

I searched on.

I crossed miles of boggy spear grass flats, soft as dough underfoot. I waded waist-deep through great stretches of brown water and its stench made my skin crawl with horror.

I had all but given up. I knew my tiger was a wise beast and would not show himself to me unless he knew he must.

For a short time I toyed with the hope that my shouts to him – where he fed with his mate – had turned him from this place.

Did I lead him to safety? I wondered. The words ran like a song inside my head. But soon they stopped and new words grew to itch at my brain.

At the edge of the rough country, where the station's green acres began, my thoughts turned sharply. As I came upon my father's snares I collected up the brush possums from the ground and carried them on my back and, suddenly, I felt a most unusual silence fall upon the bush.

I had known no silence like it in this place. I swear the breeze was told to desist. Even the marsh frogs and the tree frogs by the Myrtle burrows cut their gurglings where they lay.

I craned my neck. Stars collected like jewels in the sky as I lowered my gaze. When I shone the lantern squarely in front of me I was forced to draw in my breath sharply. It was my tiger.

He looked upon me with two steely black points, each needle eye reflecting back the lantern's light across the distance. He stood scarcely ten or twelve feet from me. I guessed his size and shape and believed he could latch his jaws on my neck in one great leap. But he did not. He merely watched me, curious.

My first thought was fear, but within a few short seconds I replaced it with a deep respect. I felt chosen by my tiger to spend time within his reach, even though I felt like a trespasser where I stood.

It appeared as plain to me then as the stars in the sky above: this island was his. I had no call to be there in his way.

My tiger faced me for a moment and then from the blackness his mate joined with him, taking his side quietly by the rear. Her eyes shone wide and welcoming; I saw no fear of me reflected in those dark pools. I watched them stand before me, quietly taking in my form, and judging me no threat. They accepted my presence in their hunting grounds.

I grew light-headed with joy, and then I caught the bull sniffing the air. He sensed the brush possum I carried on my back.

The magic I felt suddenly vanished. I wondered: was my attraction to these tigers the easy meal I carried?

I took a possum by the tail and threw it before the tigers. They watched me as if disbelieving and then the bull raised his nose to the air once more. The possum presented little interest. I tried to coax the tigers with a larger possum, edging ever nearer as I dangled the lifeless bait before them, but they were not roused.

I knew at once my actions were foolish – the tigers would not touch a dead possum – they ate only their own fresh kill.

I laid down the load I carried over my shoulder. I was now close enough to count the stripes on their backs and place the point where the fur turned downy white upon their bellies.

The tigers were beautiful creatures. They were so peaceful, and so far removed from the menacing tales that followed them to every corner of the island.

I smiled uncontrollably – my father taught me this was unwise, a predator does not like to see our teeth – but I could not hold back my joy. My happiness as this precious experience unfolded was immense.

I stood as close to the tigers as perhaps any man ever had; they held no fear of me and I held none of them. I reached out a hand before them. I wished to touch the bull's head, to feel myself closer and show my friendship. He did not recoil. I believe he would have let me touch him then, but his attention was captured and once again he raised his nose up in the air.

I withdrew my hand and with the passing of an instant, the tigers were gone, back upon their night's hunt.

I longed to go with them, to lead them far from here. To the hills and open valley spaces. To the mountain plains and the wooded gullies of the central plateau. To where there was no man to fear them. To where they could roam together in freedom, on their island home.

Chapter Twenty-Two

My mother waited by the fireside for my return. As I bounded into our crude split-paling hut the slim Huon pines burned brightly, crackling on the fire.

"Myko, you are home," she said.

I could not contain the feelings coursing through me.

"Yes, yes, Mama. I'm home again."

I felt like an excited young child, as young perhaps as when my brother and I first collected bumble bees in jam jars.

I could not chase out these thoughts of my brother. I longed to have him back. I wanted to see his smiling face and share with him the joys I felt at meeting my tiger again in the wild.

He was still my brother, we had shared so much and thoughts of him jabbed at my heart like an iron pike.

As I looked on at my mother, retreated in the shadows, I knew she too still felt deeply for Jurgis. My brother was once as much a part of us as a left hand is to the right. His memory fell upon us both as hard as a glass bottle upon a cold stone floor.

"You must be hungry, Myko," said Mother, "sit down and rest, I will prepare some food."

Mother made tea in a billycan and fired the stove for our dinner pot. Before the fire I watched her skin take on the colour of salmon flesh. Her lips twisted and her brows creased. Her shoulders rounded over where she stood. I could not believe this was my mother, who once stood as straight as a plumb-line.

"Are you all right, Mother?"

She kept her attention on the stove, "I am fine, Myko."

"You look tired. Have you been thinking of the Sakiai?"

Mother gently placed her spoon on the stove's edge. "A little, perhaps." There was a sadness in her voice. It was as if she felt trapped here, bound up as surely as an insect in a spider's web.

"I often think of our old home," I told her.

"It is natural."

"The Sakiai is a very different place to the island."

My mother was still, and then she began to speak once more. "The island is a beautiful place."

"But …" I was too eager to answer her; my mother turned to look at me. "Nothing," I said.

"You find many things to blind you to the island's beauty, Myko, I know. There are things you should not be blind to, though."

"What do you mean, Mama?"

My mother turned towards the window and looked out over the pastures and then, up towards the sky. "The wild colonials have rooted over the land like a pig's snout, seeking out the best selections for themselves. But just because they give no more thought to the island than a river does to its banks during times of flood, does not mean *we* must live this way, Myko."

I felt my chest rising and falling. I knew I was not yet blind to all the island's beauty. Tigers still roamed here and though they were as unwelcome as burrowing rodents in the settlers' veins, they still held my heart.

Suddenly I was shaken out of my thoughts by a loud rapping on the door of our hut. My mother hurriedly turned from the stove. "What is the matter? Your father, Myko, is it your father?"

"It could be anything, Mama," I said, "it does not need to be bad news."

I watched my mother take the dinner pot from the stove and quickly run to open the door. Before her, in the dark night, stood one of the station's boys. It was the carter's help, a thin and slope-shouldered youth of no more than thirteen. His pale and waxy skin caught the light of the fire's glow, turning his broad forehead to a shining yellow flatstone.

"What is it?" my mother asked him.

The boy paused for a moment as if to weigh my mother's words and then he spoke with the Tasmanian drawl I had become so familiar with. "Please, mam, I have turned up to collect the tiger man's rifle." His words came out quick and clear. As he spoke he turned and waved to the carter who waited for him outside, resting a nosebag over the carthorse and stamping out the cramps in his legs.

My mother stood motionless for a full minute. It seemed like she misunderstood the request and hoped for it to be repeated once more, but then she turned to face me.

Her narrow eyes lit up like two ripe blackberries, shining unnaturally in our dim hut. She searched me for a reaction, but as my face flushed hot with blood I froze where I stood.

I did not know what to think. Time stilled to a trickle.

Through the open door the air came sharp with the horse's odour. I heard the creek crying over the rocks and watched as the carter removed his hat to fill with water for quenching the beast's thirst.

How could it be amidst such a prosaic sight that I saw my mother reach above her to the shelf, then take down a rough sack to unfurl before the boy? I did not believe what I was seeing. I raised myself and ran to my mother, snatching the sack from her hands.

"Tell me now what he wants with this," I said.

My mother and the boy stopped still where they stood. My mother's raised hands lay open in the air like weighing scales.

I gripped the sack and twisted it tightly in my hands – my father's repeater rifle was tucked inside.

My mother's eyes shone deep with intent as she snatched

the rifle back from me and quickly handed it over to the boy.

"Here," she said, "now go."

I turned to face the boy. I grabbed hold of his thin shoulders and raked him in. "Tell me what he wants it for!"

I watched his face grow careworn, I was close enough to see the liquorice stains around his mouth.

"I'm on an errand," he said, his voice quivering, "for the tiger man."

My mother intervened: "Myko, leave him be," she said, as she took my hands from the boy and walked him indoors. Mother handed the boy an apple from her market basket as she began to fill a burlap sack with provisions for my father.

I watched as she quietly moved about our home, collecting Father's items and making forlorn glances towards me.

"What does he want with the rifle?" I said once more through my gritted teeth; the words came out louder than I intended and startled the boy.

My mother answered for him: "It is for your father, Myko, not the boy. What business is it of his!"

I felt a burst of heat deep inside my chest, my mind turned like a cartwheel; I raged, "*Why?* Why does he need it?"

Neither my mother nor the boy answered me.

I felt my brows drop low on my forehead and my eyes twist into thin creases as I viewed the pair before me. Anger coiled in me like a black snake ready to strike.

"I asked *why?*" I roared.

I did not get an answer and I reached for the rifle again; it was tight within the boy's grasp and I fought hard to wrest it from him.

"Why does he need it?" I bellowed, "*Why?*"

The boy stood dumb and silent. He seemed to be willing words to come to his mouth but they remained corked within the bottle of his mind.

A long silence fell on the hut and then a low humming sound began to build – I traced it to my mother.

Before me she stood with her hands raised up to her ears, her fingers poking in the air like jagged reed spikes, and then she screamed out: "*Stop! Stop! Stop this now!*"

My mother's voice drawled slowly over her careful words as she stared on at me. "Myko, what is wrong?" Her voice seared into me. But I cared nothing for what she had to say.

I pushed the boy beyond my reach and lashed out at the wall, bringing down a row of shelving. Pothooks and plates crashed on the floor.

I lost all control of my actions as an evil threatening whispered reminders of the tiger skins I had seen my father peg on the trees around our home. I would not allow him to lay a hand on my tiger's coat.

"Get him out my sight," I roared.

I sensed my tiger's time was close to running out.

Chapter Twenty-Three

I watched my mother, stooped before me in our crude split-paling hut, collecting up the tin plates and pothooks I had scattered on the floor. Her shoulders tensed, her face seemed as if it were smeared with a thick white oil. "I dreamt of the *takmakas* again last night," she said quietly.

Mother watched me beneath hooded eyes; she looked tired. "Dreams often come to me of the Sakiai."

Nightmares had assailed my mother for weeks. She spoke of them on many occasions. I knew she still gave great store to the old ways, to the superstitions and the wives' tales. To my mother, every action bore a hidden meaning, a second consequence to be understood. The way the goats gave milk or how quickly wood burned on the fire foretold some action yet to come; especially misfortunes that may yet befall us.

In the silence between us I listened to the hearth's hiss. As I turned my head to look upon my mother, my breath came light and regular and I chose my words with caution. "Was it the same dream?" I asked.

My mother's voice was stiff. "Yes. I am forever dreaming of it now."

I felt myself sink back where I sat. I locked my fingers over my chest. "I have lots of dreams which come time and again," I told my mother, "it does not mean anything." I wanted to distract her but seemed only to draw her derision.

"Myko," she said curtly, her words cutting me down, "I do not believe you have learned much of our old ways!"

It grew warm in our hut now. The logs burned high within the fire's grate and the flames played on the walls like dancing gypsies. My mother looked so forlorn, so tired. She curled a knitted shawl around her thin shoulders; her bones poked beneath the heavy woollen folds like poles under canvas. Her facial muscles twitched nervously. Her strange code of morals weighed her down.

"We have failed to show you the right and proper ways, Myko, have we not?"

I tried to gain her attention once again; I wanted to shift the talk away from this subject. "I will fix up the shelves now," I said.

My mother did not listen to my words. Her voice changed, took on a low, almost faint tone. I believe it carried defeat. "Your father was in the dream again, Myko."

I knew at once why she seemed so agitated.

As my mother lowered herself slowly into the chair by the fireside, I moved over to sit before her. I sensed her presence slipping farther and farther away. Her thin body tensed and her eyes burned like candle wicks before me.

I knew there was only one subject that would engage her now. I faced it like a high granite ledge, a mountain between us, which I knew my mother called me to climb.

I felt the sweat beading on my brow as I spoke. "And the wolves?" The words scratched at my throat as they came.

Mother shifted uncomfortably where she sat, she glowered up at me and her face became a mask of torture; "They were tigers ... and he carried no *takmakas!*"

I looked at my mother's ashen face; where she sat she seemed to repel all the fire's warmth. I did not try to engage her again, I believed I was naïve to try at all. I felt the breath in my lungs seeping slowly out, taking with it any words I might have said, had I any inside me to make better such a matter.

I watched my mother bunch up her expression. Heavy lines crossed her face, she gritted her teeth and they became as hard as picket pins driven down into the ground. "Do you know, Myko, in the olden days, there was the cholera," she indicated

138

with her thumb over her shoulder, in the direction of the past, "how precious our sleep was then."

My mother leaned away from me and tried to warm her bony hands by the fire. I could feel her deep sadness creep within me; I wished I could see a better life for her. My poor mother, I wished for nothing more than to see her return to the brief happiness we shared in the Sakiai – when Jurgis was with us – when my father worked the farm and we were all a family, together.

Mother crouched closer to the fire and drew her shawl tighter. She swayed gently to and fro as if taken by a trance. She began to talk in a voice that did not seem to be hers. "My Myko," she called out to me, "when the cholera was with us they said a lady in black rode a carriage pulled by four black horses in the night."

My eyes grew wider. I felt alert as a cat, listening to my mother.

"I want to know about the lady," I said.

Mother smiled, her lips widened for an instant, and then as fast as rain splashes down from the heavens her smile was gone again, replaced by the dark vault that returned echoes of our past. "The lady carried a tarred whip above her head," she said, "and when she came upon a village or a farmhouse she cracked the whip upon a windowpane and cried out, 'Are you sleeping?'"

I watched my mother's words form on her cold mouth. I heard the wind moving in the treetops outside, but the view that seized my gaze sat before me. At once I felt myself drawn again to my mother's tales.

"Inside," said Mother, "beyond the window's pane, if there was a reply of 'No', then all would be well. The household survived the cholera. But if the people were sleeping and nobody replied, then … the next morning they were all found dead!"

139

Mother paused, she took a deep breath and steadied her voice. "As she withdrew from the window, Cholera said, 'If it is asleep you are – then go on sleeping'!"

I looked again upon my mother where she sat, swaying gently before the fire. I saw a look of reverie in her eye, a sparkle which slowly changed. It turned into a tear, slipped over her cheek and then it ran down the length of her face.

"My Myko, when I was a girl, to protect us from Cholera I stayed awake in the night. In each and every house in the Sakiai, one person did this, so that when Cholera came riding we called out, '*We are not asleep! We are not asleep!*' at the top of our lungs."

She became agitated again. I watched my mother wipe away tears with the back of her hand. Her whole arm trembled as though she hammered at an anvil. I reached out and held fast to her. "But, Mother," I said, "we have no cholera here."

My mother turned her face from me and I saw more tears following the others that appeared on her pale face. "No, my Myko," she said, "and we have none of the old ways to protect us."

Chapter Twenty-Four

I left my mother rocking by the fire. I tried to rest, but sleep evaded me. I feared Mother would lose sleep also, and that the deprivation would harm her. I knew she longed for my father's return to cosset and protect him like she always had done, but I knew there must be conflict when Father showed.

My mind moved again and again to thoughts of Father pursing my tiger. Like a river washing over the same bed of rocks I felt unable to halt this course, or even influence how it might unfold.

I imagined, in detail, what might befall my tiger. The images seemed so real that I smelled the burning of my tiger's wounds, where Father's bullets would enter, scorching the fur and flesh.

I rose and stalked the hut in rage.

Sinful thoughts blazed inside me. It shamed me to think I might take against my own father. I longed to kick out, to tear down the walls, but I could not.

I sank to the floor and lay clutching at my stomach. My pains felt real, they rose like angry waves in my gut. Then I grew unsure; is it *my* sin? Will I not be doing God's work? I wondered. The thought woke me like the morning's goat-bells and I stood to pace the floor once more.

To think of challenging my father, of attacking his duty, made my blood run cold as the water in the rocky brook. Father's duty maintained his last stores of pride, it was the badge of his manhood, and it kept us from hunger. As my thoughts turned over, I was surprised to find myself breathing as calmly as ever I had.

In the heavy moving blackness of the night I felt ready to cast out my father's grim trade. I would hurl all he stood for from the clifftops to the jagged rock crops below, and hang the consequences.

My only shame was that my mother might suffer. For myself I was prepared to be left with nothing, but I could see my mother suffered already. I knew she was wracked with fear. She succumbed to her own superstitions; her nightmares have brought her near to ruin, I thought.

As I returned to my crib, I saw how little attention I had paid to Mother's traditions. I no longer called myself a child of the old county. The island seeped within me, its ragged shores and button grass plains were now my inner boundary, as surely as my mother's was the lush winding valleys of the Sakiai.

I believed I had no place for the old world now. I felt somewhere far from such things. I felt no fear of *Giltine*.

I watched the morning's light begin to break outside the window of our crude split-paling hut. The green of the paddocks rose up as the hard silver of the gumposts reflected the early beams of light.

The air outside was still and pure without the hum of insects. Even the rippling stream's down-curved path moved silently towards the headwaters of the river. I felt at peace until, suddenly, dark thoughts crowded my mind.

I had a sudden sense of another presence within our small settler's shack. The smell of the tar which sealed the roof beams disappeared and was replaced by a muskier, stronger scent. I felt my pulse quicken where I lay, but I could not move. My mind seemed somehow trapped within my body, fixed on thoughts which surely were not real.

I felt the wind blowing from the coast. It came beneath the door, then suddenly I was pulled upright, as if a string attached to my chest was quickly jerked tight. As I stared at the door I felt the wind pressed from outside.

We kept only a weak hasp on the hut's door. In high gales its pin blew out. As I gazed on, the pin began to twitch; it shivered like an icicle preparing to fall and then it rocked violently for a moment, before snapping like a dry twig.

I could not move as the door slowly opened into the hut. I felt my mouth shut so tightly that I feared words would never again pass my lips. I watched in disbelief as a flat, snub nose sniffed beyond the door's jamb. It traced the scent of something but appeared wary in unknown territory.

I kept my gaze on the snout until the beast's form grew before me and, finally, it revealed itself in the morning light.

The animal stood in full view.

Its back was straight and true; each black stripe of its coat shone as dark as ravens' wings.

It stood before me like the island's king.

I did not believe what I saw, as I watched my tiger walking on the boards of our hut.

As I gazed upon my tiger, where he stood before me, his dark eyes contained little joy. I saw the fawn patches on his coat twitching, he looked anxious. He lifted his great snout to the air and I feared he might howl before me like a wolf.

Beyond the door's swish the wind suddenly lulled inside the hut. As I watched my tiger moving I was close enough to feel the fetch and miss of his breath. My heart stilled. I raised myself on the bunk's edge and turned to see my mother slumped in sleep. I knew that if she woke to find my tiger, my father would be at hunt before dawn.

Slowly, I lowered myself over the crib's edge and stood up. I was silent but my tiger sensed me. He scratched at the boards before him and let out long, heavy grunts that came from deep inside his hollow chest.

His neck muscles rose and tensed, and then his shoulder blades straightened. His flank now filled the length of the hut as he faced me down.

It felt like extracting a thorn, watching my tiger stand in

fear of me. I wanted him to see our paths were merged, that together we were one, like the sand in the sea.

I moved to raise my hand and then, slowly, as I reached out to him I watched my tiger turn from me. He had little space to move about and a bony lump of flesh gathered like an ant-hill on his back.

My tiger was uneasy. He lowered his neck like a pack hound before it strikes and I recoiled my hand at once.

Quickly, but quietly and with little fuss, my tiger made to leave.

For the instant that he stood atop the hearth-rug his glossy coat was umber-coloured in the fire's dim glow; he placed an eye on me, then he darted and was gone.

At once I ran behind him. My heart pounded heavily. The morning light blurred my eyes but I could see my tiger was glad to have his freedom. He managed his steps with precision and gave no way to fallen bough or dray in the yard. I watched him clear our stone wall in one flighty leap. And then he vanished from sight.

Where did he go? Will he come back?

I knew I had my chance now to lead him from this place.

I loped after my tiger like an ape. The path was churned and caked-over where the flocks had crossed and I stumbled. The stirring mosquitos pestered me where I fell, but I caught sight of my tiger by a sassafras tree for an instant. I watched as he broke into a short, slow trot across the coastal heathland and I quickly fastened tight my bluchers and made after him.

Where I ran, shy New Holland mice scattered at my feet. My tiger headed beyond the flowering milkmaids and wild violets towards the forest's edge. As we reached the thick covering of the bush I kept pace with him. Now and again he turned his head towards me, sometimes raising up his snout to the air. I was careful to keep from his sight, but I wondered, does he know I follow?

My tiger knew every inch of these woodlands. I could not mistake his home-range for that of any man. It was thick with mighty eucalypts and pines; beneath them the rain-specked man ferns and ragged purple appleberry bushes scrapped at my legs as I followed him deeper into this strange new place.

I watched him crouch low in the shadows of the canopy and beneath the outcroppings of rock and rotting branches that lay before us on the forest floor. My tiger moved swiftly and yet he stalked these pitted tracks and muddy waterholes as though he were the hunted. I sensed his fear like it was my own.

My tiger's slow track through the darkness beneath the canopy was a nervy one. I saw he was a timid beast. The tiger of legend – the demon, hunted – was no more a creature to be feared than any stumbling wombat or a blowfly trapped within a bottle.

My tiger made no noise and yet I was filled with the words he did not say. I sensed his every move. I ran behind him through the wooded plains and thickets like I had run with him all my life.

We're running from something, I thought. I do not know why or how I knew this, I just felt it seep into me, as clear as a damp bark roof steaming under the hot sun.

Soon my tiger slowed. His steps turned to a peaceful trot and he stopped still. Where he stood, as I stared on feeling my breath return to normal, I saw my tiger clearly.

The light was fully up now and I took in the sun-streaked flashes of his coat. He raised his snub nose to the air once more and the whiskers either side of his snout twitched straight. And then, out of the dense scrub beyond my tiger's gaze, stepped his mate.

My tiger continued a few feet towards her and then, as he

stopped short of her, his mate took the extra steps to greet him with her head and tail lowered.

I felt the air come sharp and cold in my nostrils, it carried the tigers' heavy scent as sweetly as cinnamon to my senses. My tiger's mate was long-legged and agile looking and she emitted a low and happy yip. Beneath her belly I saw the swell of her pouch – she now carried young. Her pouch was smooth and rounded. Soon these newborn tigers would be walking among us.

I watched the scene unfold before my eyes with wonder. "Did my tiger bring me here, to the depths of the forest?" I asked myself, "has he shown me his own sacred lair?"

As I watched the tigers together I saw that in this one last remote hide they had defied their tormentors. There were many hands turned against them and yet their will, their need to survive, won through.

But as I looked upon my tiger and his mate, I understood they now had nowhere left to run. Were their cubs to survive they would need more than my tiger's protection. I wanted to believe he had come to me for help.

Chapter Twenty-Five

My mother bore much in the Sakiai for my brother and me. Her darkest times were like an ogre-tale we all lived through. But on New Year's morning when Pranciskis woke us to check the branches we had placed in the snow, to tell our fortunes, I feared the worst was yet to come.

All the branches stood upright, except for one – my mother's. As her wan eyes drank in the scene she cried, but spoke no words.

"Do not fear," said Pranciskis, "it is my branch more than yours."

Mother grabbed my brother, and I stood close to her and stared into her face, wet with tears. I felt like I was looking deep into her, staring at the very soul of my mother, at the one piece of her that she felt sure she still possessed.

She gathered the fold-creases of her shawl; "But, it was my branch."

Pranciskis placed a bony finger on her forearm. "Did I not plant it in the snow for you?" he said. "It was my hands that touched it and not yours."

Mother wept. Her tears ran in slow driblets down her face; both she and I knew Pranciskis only tried to win her favour. He offered out his open hand and my mother took it.

At once my brother tugged at my shirtsleeve and pointed to our mother and Pranciskis as they joined before us. I shrugged off Jurgis where he pulled at me. I felt a tight knot come to my stomach once again. It turned and twisted like a bolt-screw with each breath I took.

As I watched my brother withdraw from me I looked back to my mother. I wanted to shout to her, *'Put down Pranciskis's hand right away!'* But I did not. I dared not utter a single word. I did not want to hear my mother tell me once again that it must be this way.

I knew that I had learned something, because I now wondered what choice she had.

The sun shone high above our heads as Pranciskis stood proud in the yard. He held his arms out from his chest, his hands were open wide to their fingertips. He denied his crippled leg where he stood, like a whole man.

"The coming year will be a prosperous one," said Pranciskis, "yes, I can see we will have great fortunes this year."

As he smiled at my mother and repeated his prediction, I knew anything less would be an affront to Pranciskis's new stores of pride.

In the months that followed we all put in together, preparing the land and tilling the soil in readiness of the crops. Pranciskis toiled with us on the farm, but we knew he did not care much for our work.

He cut short his labours. "How can this be all there is for me?" he called out, "I have more to give this land than my sweat!"

Pranciskis came from the same peasant stock as Kazimeras and Ruta, but his pride made him speak this way; I knew he dreamed of higher things for himself.

"I must leave," said Pranciskis. He threw down the long handle of his hoe and went, with his strange hirple, across the fields, bleating: "My leg ails me."

I looked at my brother and he shook his head. Even Jurgis saw that Pranciskis feigned this ailment.

By day's end the sun had all but settled. The sky kept a dark hue throughout, but at its far reaches a lavender-colour lingered, throwing down just enough light to guide us on our path home.

We walked silently, tired out but satisfied from our labours. We each wore dark faces, blackened with soil. Around our eyes clear white circles showed where we had kept the grime from our sight.

As Kazimeras opened the door I saw Pranciskis sitting in Father's chair at the table, smoking a pipe. Mother cleared dishes from the table and delicately swept bread crumbs into her apron at Pranciskis's side.

"Daina, Daina, stop with that," said Pranciskis, "bring food for the labourers … my brother, are you not hungry?"

Kazimeras nodded and Pranciskis motioned him to sit at his side. We ate together and round the table there was quiet, save for Pranciskis's little speeches.

"I should have been an officer in the Russian Army by now, don't you know," he said to us boys. "Yes, yes … it was to be my calling."

Pranciskis leaned towards us and twirled his carefully waxed mustachios, cultivated in the style of the Czar's generals. I believe he wished us to respond to his speech, but my brother and I sat motionless, our hands beneath our legs. We had no interest in his stories. We hoped Pranciskis would soon leave us and return to his pipe and books, the books which were in Russian, and filled with such reveries for him.

Pranciskis stood up sharply. "Very well," he said. He turned from us at the table and began to pound the heavy boards as he walked around us.

A great thud was suddenly sounded as Pranciskis brought down his bony fist on the table; the pots and plates shook where they stood. "You do not know what it is to keep a man from his proper duty!" he yelled.

My brother and I sat before him in silence; we both heard his heavy breathing and smelled the tobacco smoke on his clothing. "Go, go from my sight," he roared at us.

We answered his command as though marching to a bugle call in his parade; quickly we ran to our room.

After some time my brother and I strayed from our keep. From atop the staircase we peered between the balusters together.

"Why does Mama not come to us?" said Jurgis.

"That is why, look," I said, pointing.

Beneath us we spied our mother and Pranciskis together. Mother sat by his side, rising only to stoke the fire and light thin wooden tapers for his pipe. Our mother listened patiently and smiled sweetly, averting her gaze when Pranciskis's temper rose and he delivered an outburst.

As my mother turned from him, Pranciskis placed a hand beneath her chin and returned her gaze to him. He was in constant demand of Mother's attention. Every day, it seemed, Pranciskis grew more pampered and lazy.

"Why does she stay there with him?" said Jurgis.

I had no answer for my brother.

"Mama does not want to come to us!" My brother was angry. His mouth became twisted as he watched our mother below us, with Pranciskis. "I hate *him*," said Jurgis, "*I hate him. I hate him.*"

"I do too," I said. My answer came quickly; it required little of my thought.

I wanted to run. I wanted to run far, far away. I dreamed of finding a new home, like the boy in fairytales who packs his goods in a kerchief, and sets off alone into the forest. But I could not leave my mother and brother.

And then, when our fortunes seemed at their lowest, when all hope had long since passed and our days stretched before us like the frozen Nemunas and the icy pastures, my brother broke the morning stillness with an unearthly cry.

"Look! Look, Myko," he roared.

Jurgis awoke the entire household, but I was the first to see my brother's excitement. He pressed his face hard against the windowpane, the cold moisture of its surface sticking flat his blond fringe.

"Look, Myko, look," he said from atop the sill where he sat.

Jurgis spoke frantically, he had no shortage of words. It was as if the riverbanks of my brother's mind had suddenly burst and their torrent was in full flow.

"Brother, *please*," he said, pointing urgently through the window to the fields and woods below.

I followed his excited gaze and I looked out. I stared and stared, but I saw nothing unusual save the heavy frost and the little silver wands hanging from the branches, which tinkled with the silent breeze.

"Jurgis," I said, "I see nothing."

My brother grabbed onto my head; his fingers clasped me tightly as he pointed my eyes to the far distance.

"There," he said, "look, there, there!"

It was plain my brother had stronger eyes than me.

"Do you see?" he asked, "do you see?"

I picked up some movement. "I see … something," I said. "You do?"

"Yes," I said. I found it hard to make out what I saw. "But what is it? Is it a man?"

Our mother came quickly into our room. Pranciskis trailed behind her, his watery blue eyes rolled up behind his long girl's lashes as he tried to divine what occupied us so.

"Come now, what is all this commotion?" he said. "It is barely morning, do you expect us to rise before the cockcrow?"

He pushed us aside and took in the view.

The hair at the back of Pranciskis's head stood up as straight as hitching-posts from where he had lain with our mother. His small hook of a nose touched the glass like the beak of a pigeon scratching for breadcrumbs from a kindly widow, one who welcomes such company daily, and gives in to such demanding ways.

Jurgis stood silent beside Pranciskis and lowered his head; he was bowed before Pranciskis, but not with fear. My brother was barely ten years old and already more a man than this lame, weak and vain fool who blighted our lives. It was the shame of seeing Pranciskis standing by our mother, she and him in their bedclothes, together before us, which wounded Jurgis.

"You discovered this?" said Pranciskis to my brother.

I watched Jurgis nod as Pranciskis turned back to the window.

"Good boy, good boy," he said.

A smile spread over my brother's face, but I saw that he cared not an ounce for the praise he received.

Pranciskis stood back from the sill and excitedly ran from our room, his buckled bones showing beneath his nightclothes. As he went I saw my cunning brother had taken league with the Devil, his smile turning quickly to a wicked smirk of glee.

In the short time that followed our home became suddenly taken by a great flurry. Mostly it was fuelled by Pranciskis, who hopped quickly on his one good leg from room to room, commanding us.

Kazimeras and Ruta stood puzzled before their excited relative. The peasants' lower lips, it seemed to me, hung like dumb packhounds' jowls around their necks.

"Quick, move yourselves," said Pranciskis, "do you want the entire Russian Army to know we live like pigs?"

Pranciskis went to sit at the table's head, facing the door, behind one of his military books. Mother quickly lit his pipe for him with a taper from the fire, whilst the rest of us did his bidding – moving about straightening the wall mounts, putting fresh apples in baskets and piling up logs by the fire.

I watched Jurgis happily shift about the room, dancing like a wildflower in high wind. He knew something more than the rest of us about the Russian soldier who slowly wended his way through the frost towards our home.

As I peered through the little red window shutters with the heart-shape cut out in the middle I saw only a stooped, slowly moving figure clad head to toe in the army's green serge. Even the soldier's face was shrouded behind scarves. It seemed as though the conditions outside represented a deadly threat to his health.

My brother and I wanted to run to the soldier but Mother did not allow it. Even though to us all, as he neared our door, the soldier seemed a pitiable figure, gripping to his walking stick and swaying with the slightest of a breeze.

Pranciskis roared: "Be seated, both of you. You will wait out your turn. It will be me the soldier wishes to address first, surely."

Pranciskis's eyes grew wild when he spoke, his tone reached higher than usual and his manners became agitated. He was an animated little terrier tied by a rabbit hole, unable to hold for his release.

We all waited for the soldier to knock, but he did not.

The soldier merely walked right in through the door, and why not? It was our home, and he was our father.

Chapter Twenty-Six

When I returned home I found my tiger's footprints everywhere. My breath quickened as I kicked fresh earth over the most visible tracks and smoothed over the ground where my tiger had been.

"The tiger's print is most specific, it cannot be confused with any other animal, even a dog," my father had once told me.

His words came back ringing in my ears. I had asked him to show me, so I might be able tell a tiger print. "The arrangement of the toes and claws is quite different … look, Myko."

My father showed the tiger's two clefts in the rear of its pad. "The dog does not have these clefts, Myko. It is a simple track to follow."

No one who knows a tiger print could ever mistake it for anything else. I knew at once my father would soon latch upon my tiger's markings. The thought of him returning to find these tracks so close to home set my heart crossways.

I worked hurriedly, but I knew that my actions were in vain – Father's dogs would surely scent my tiger's presence. At a point so close to the dogs' own territory, where they fed and had marked as their own, there would be mayhem roused by my tiger's showing.

My only hope was for Father to return heavily burdened after the dipping so that his exhaustion forced him to seek rest at once. If this happened, then perhaps my tiger would be merely chased on by Father's dogs.

"Dogs will not attack a tiger on their own." My father's words followed me as I rubbed and rubbed at the dry earth.

We once spoke freely; "Why not?" I had asked him.

"A tiger can cause great fear in a dog," said Father, "a dog must be taught to attack a tiger and, even then, coaxed into every conflict."

"The dogs are frightened of the tigers? Why?"

My father had lowered his gaze, his eyes bored into me with an intensity I still recalled. "They fear what they do not know, Myko," he said.

I got down on my knees and swept at the tiger tracks with the flat of my hand. Dread filled me, but more of my father's words came back to give me hope that my tiger could be spared one last fight.

I remembered the time Nathaniel suggested to my father they go snaring near the plains to seek out winter furs. My father dismissed the rugged trek to the island's deepest reaches.

"I know of no one who has settled there," he said, "the land offers nothing to man."

It sounded like an adventure to me. I needed to know why he refused Nathaniel. "Why? What is there?" I asked.

"The island's interior has heavy rainfall, Myko. Much of the country is elevated and covered with thick forests. The mountain tops are craggy and the gullies deep and wide. Access to these regions is difficult for any man."

"Nobody goes there?"

"Even the hardiest bushcutters find the undisturbed terrain too tough."

"Then why did the idea excite Nathaniel so much?"

My father shook his head. I did not know whether it was my question or Nathaniel's suggestion he found most naïve. "To the island's native species, the interior is a haven," he said, "the pademelons and devils occur there in great numbers. The possums thrive too. But it is no place for man, Myko."

The island held many places where no man could access the land, where the swamp gums reached three-hundred feet high. Places of poor climate and mountain cirques that are impossible to farm. This kind of land is of no use to any man.

In such a place, I now wondered, could my tiger be safe?

My hands were covered with the red earth. The layers beneath the topsoil were dry and scorched at my palms, but I continued to rub away at my tiger's tracks, lost in my thoughts.

I knew there was great fear of unsettled regions in this part of the world. The settler's lore was scattered with tales of men who perished far from home. Some succumbed to hunger, others merely lost to nature in the bleak land.

Mile upon mile of desert on the main is said to be littered with the remains of early settlers who sought riches beyond the sand dunes. Others merely tried to challenge the further reaches of the unknown, and perished for their curiosity.

Between the elements, the natives, and nature's snakes and spiders, a yellow streak of cowardice was painted around much of the land by superstitious fools. Such regions just might be my tiger's saviour.

If I could lead him far from his lair, I thought, then with his mate and cubs, he could be at peace.

In the island's heart my tiger would find rest, content that the hunter he feared most had no desire to intrude upon him there.

As I withdrew from the ground I looked down at my hands to see my blood mixed with the red of the earth. Dark welts curled around the smoother parts of the flesh which had swelled and turned the colour of raw meat. I was aware of the pain I had caused myself as I rubbed my damaged hands together.

Slowly, I walked to the water pump. I brought down the heavy handle several times and the cool water which flowed out soothed my nagging wounds. I could not so easily alter the course of my thoughts.

I pushed my head beneath the pump's spout. The flow of water flattened the thick crop of my yellow hair and ran down on my back. My clothes clung to me, my shirt was soaked with the cool water, and I shivered where I stood.

As I withdrew from the water pump I found my mind had not altered; my thoughts remained the same. Where I stood, on my father's tied holding, was not a place my tiger should be. If he stayed he would be killed as surely as if I were to seize a scope gun and train its sights on him.

I returned indoors where, in the hut's stuffy stench, I found my mother sleeping. She looked peaceful, deep inside her dreams. My mother was far from me; I wondered what occupied her thoughts in her deep sleep. She looked like a small child, curled in her bed, smiling at all the happy goings of another world.

My mother was content, yet for such a long time she had been assailed by cruelties in her sleep. This morning the demons lifted from her, as fast as a bushfire cleared by heavy rain. I longed to keep Mother within my gaze for as long as I could, but as I watched the face that only moments before had been kissed by angels, my mother turned suddenly as grey as the ash on a funeral pyre.

Mother's head jerked back violently and she sat bolt upright, her mouth agape before me. "Myko!" she called out.

I stood before her, but she looked through me as if I were glass. "Mama, I'm here," I said. My words sounded clear but my mother was wracked by spasms of fear where she sat, bead-eyed and hollow-cheeked.

"Myko, Myko," she cried out again.

"Yes, I'm here."

My mother snapped from her trance and held me in her gaze. "Oh, my Myko, my Myko," she said. Her voice was stilled and mouse-like.

I held my arms out to her. I knew she dreamt again of my father's death to come. I saw the familiar scene which played

157

upon her face at such times.

I raised the lantern by her bed and brought more coarse-woven blankets to take away her chills.

"Be calm, Mama," I said.

I offered all the comfort I could gather, but my blood twitched within my veins at the task before me. I knew that, no matter how unwell my mother might be, I must make a hasty departure from her soon.

"Mother, I must leave you alone," I said, "I have my duties. Will you be all right?

"Oh, Myko, you are a good boy," she said.

My mother stroked my hair gently with her hand and I sensed her care for me. Though my mother's blessings were heartfelt, I wished for none of this now. I only wanted my mother to end her drill of daily hurts.

A loose curl unfurled itself from the dark frowziness of Mother's hair. I reached over to turn it behind her ear and she clasped my hand tightly, "You have become so busy, Myko … what is it?" she said.

I could not let her know what I was about. I remained icy calm.

"Mama," I said, as I pulled away from her, "I have my duties."

Mother leaned toward me and I saw that the contours of her face grew hard. Her mouth was a taut wire, her eyes grief-ravaged beyond their bemused stare. "What duties?" she said.

I did not answer; I collected my scarf and tied it before her to show I must leave quickly. Grim imaginings prowled through my thoughts. I knew my time to act was now.

"Goodbye, Mama," I said softly.

I left my mother trembling in the cold of our crude split-paling hut. As I hurried on the road, I felt a deep shame that I did not light any fire in the hearth.

158

My mother was distressed, and I had left her hastily in her time of need. I tried to push these thoughts away, but my head was filling with many dark images now. I forced myself into the task before me and I ran towards it keenly. I planned to take on only my lightest duties and then I would return home, to seek out my tiger. Beyond this I did not know what awaited me. I only knew that if I could somehow gather up my tiger and his family, I would set out for the island's rugged interior.

Chapter Twenty-Seven

It was a cold morning. As I walked my steps came as slow and light as the dew settled upon the pastures. I pulled my collars tight and tried to fix my thoughts on what I must do, but my feet felt weighted down and began to trail me.

I knew I was being foolish to take such a task upon myself. My chance of reaching the end I hoped for was slim when I had the entire station staked against me. For years the settlers had hunted the tigers in these lands. Could I really hope to save my tiger in the face of such hatred?

I crossed one of Father's stiles; its steps were wet beneath my feet and forced me to lose balance. As I fell backwards my head landed hard on the last of the steps. Where I lay, the sun's light crossed my eyes quickly and my heart was cajoled to beat a little faster. I was unhurt, but shaken.

I raised myself up and the bead of gold in the sky retreated behind a cloud. I imagined its brief appearance served to widen my eyes, and I put in hard on my path. As I strolled the pastures my boots stuck in the moist soil. Damp fronds clung at my heels and fell like petals upon the breeze as my pace quickened.

My strides grew with my purpose and I saw that to leave the station at such a busy time was wrong, but this bothered my conscience little. I had to search out my tiger, no matter where it took me. All that mattered to me at this time, as I took charge of my slim hope, was my tiger's survival.

The amber sun shone dully, its light leaking through the white clouds and breaking on the green dimness of the fields. I kept a steady eye on the down-cupped grooves of the low hills as I drifted on the track to the station.

Why should I dwell on fears? The thought grabbed me like an eerie shock. I felt my heart governed by a greater power.

A source from outside took over: my mind, my body and my actions were not my own now.

Tall trees skirted the track on both sides and swayed in the blue air above the rapid singing stream. It wasn't long until I saw the smoke spirals rising from the billet's chimney stacks and soon, as I cut through the yellow paddocks, I was close enough to hear the roof's loose shingles rattling in the breeze.

"Boy, come down this way," a man yelled to me, "this cart needs unloading."

I had hoped to avoid chores, but all the boys were being led to and from the station's billet as if part of a great procession.

"Come on, come on. The sacks won't jump down themselves," said the foreman from the bakery.

With the other boys I began to take down the heavy sackfuls piled high on the carriage floor. The foreman smiled; his voice was different from the coarseness of the other men, his words weren't strangled by a Tasmanian drawl but sounded in the proper fashion, like an Englishman.

"Well done boys," he called out, "we'll have this truck empty in no time. No time at all."

I watched the foreman flare out his nostrils and lick at his underlip, and then he joined with the great flurry of boys in unloading the truck.

We worked like demons as the foreman's voice raked the air, shouting encouragements, "Keep up, keep up boys. Many hands make light the work!"

Every boy fell mute, their heads bowed, their backs turned to the sky as they pressed into the task. I saw each boy grow swollen-faced, the blood brightening their cheeks as they worked in a trance.

"Myko, Myko," I heard my name called at me. As I moved to follow the sound, I saw Tilly watching from beyond the cart's front.

161

"What are you doing?" she said.

"I have to help out. Why aren't you helping?"

Tilly threw up her hands and then she kicked up dust with her bare feet. "You know why!"

"What?"

Tilly jumped into the cart. "Because I am a girl, silly."

I did not think I was the silly one. Tilly stood taller than me, I thought whoever stopped her from working with us boys must be the silly one.

As I bent to pick up another flour sack Tilly placed a bare foot on the load before me, "Leave it," she said, "I have something to show you."

I looked over my shoulder; I saw the other boys wondering why I had stopped working.

"Tilly, I have to help them."

She dug in her heel as I tried to pick up another sack; it was impossible to lift.

"Tilly, the foreman will see."

She pulled her hands from her pockets and latched them on my shoulders, spinning me around to face the mill's coign; "Open your eyes, Myko!"

I saw the foreman stood with a crowd of settlers, his long bony fingers digging into his tobacco pouch as he smiled and laughed with the group of men.

I straightened my back and took a step closer, to stand staring, unblinking. Flies clustered in my nostrils and eyes as I halted and I felt my shirt clinging to me.

"Come on, Myko, let's go."

My breathing came in gasps as I stepped down from the cart. The boys watched as I went, but did not halt in their labours. I walked soundlessly, all the while staring back to the boys, until I reached the water barrel and quenched my thirst.

Tilly leaned on the water barrel and kicked out her legs as I drank. She wore a white flannel shirt that was torn at one elbow and covered with pale bluebells. "I know something that you don't, Myko," she said. I knew she was trying to tease me with this new knowledge of hers.

"What is it?"

Tilly leaned away from the barrel and tipped back her head. She looked up to the sky as she spoke, with one finger tapping the side of her face. "Oh, just that the grey mare is stabled up."

At this time the grey worked harder than ever; I found it impossible to believe. "In the stable? Why?"

"Never mind why, Myko, come on." Tilly set out running for the stable. I followed behind her, wondering what we would find. I knew the animal was not sick, Tilly would have been upset by such news, but I wondered why the mare was not put to work.

At the stables the grey stuck out her nose and shook her mane up and down at the sight of us. Tilly ran forward and, leaning on her toes, stroked the mare's face. She smiled widely as the beast's ears twitched happily.

"Look, she's glad to see us," said Tilly.

I stood at Tilly's back and watched as she harnessed up the grey and led it out into the paddock. "Here, Myko, you can go first," she said.

I took the reins from Tilly. "But why has the grey been left in the stable today?" I asked.

Tilly did not seem interested in my question. "Oh, the men rose early today, that's probably why."

"Risen early, for the dipping?" I asked.

"No, Myko, they're finished."

If the dipping was finished I understood why the mare was stabled. But surely the men would be at rest in the early morning if there was no dipping? "Tilly, where are the men now?"

163

She lifted her hand to the grey's flank. "Up, up, Myko. Come on, we have the horse all day!"

"Tilly, the men, where are they?" I pressed.

She turned away from me and patted at the grey. "Should I go first? Do you not want to take your turn?"

I placed a hand on Tilly's shoulder and gently moved her towards me. "Tilly, tell me."

Tilly dropped her head before me; I thought she might start to cry.

"Tilly, what is the matter?"

"Oh, Myko," she began to sob.

I touched her face, it was wet with tears.

"Myko, I don't want to say."

As I looked at Tilly I felt her anguish; between us the air was thick with her hurt. I did not need to hear her say the words she held inside. I climbed onto the grey and dug in my heels.

"Myko! Myko!" I heard Tilly calling at my back, but I was already across the paddock and pressing the grey hard on the road.

Many thoughts scratched at my mind. I felt as if some tiny burrowing rodent, a spotted quoll perhaps, or an eager bandicoot, had climbed in my ear and refused to leave until it explored every last inch of my head.

Upon the grey's back I grew both hot and cold, I felt like a fever had overcome me. My heart beat both fast and slow as I took the horse out into the pastures around Woolnorth to search for my father, but I could not see him anywhere.

In the fields the flocks huddled quietly under the blue and cloud-washed sky. I found no hint of any threat to them from the tigers my father was employed to rid the station of.

I followed the road through the heat haze and beyond the wall of trees that jutted the heathland like a giant-cut wedge. The grey felt sprightly and eager and I allowed her to stretch out her legs in a gallop for a time. When the grey's breath hardened I clawed in the reins and her pace slowed enough for me to see the magpies probing the trees' bark on the ground for insects.

I soon came to a sturdy fencepost, where I spotted an old cove. I nodded first and then removed my cap; its cloth was dampened with the sweat of my brow and I wrung it in my hands like twisting hay. "Mr Coyle," I said, acknowledging his name.

The old cove's face shone like a lantern and his honey-coloured whiskers leaped up his face like nimble squirrels. As he began to speak through a wide palate, his tongue roamed so freely that his words broke like steamer whistles.

"Is a fine day for roaming the pastures, my young man," he said. His every utterance came sheathed with whistles and sprays. "But it's a queer sort of place this morning … very quiet, very quiet indeed."

"Have you seen my father?" I asked.

The old cove surveyed me from head to toe, he seemed perturbed that I interrupted his claver.

"Oh, the tiger man? I saw him," he said. He became excited and a loud clack replaced his whistles, it sounded like the noise of a platypus diving on calm waters. "I saw many men this morning!"

I knew the old cove was keeping coy. For some time I had known that to men like him there was great sport to be had from my clumsy grasp of the island's rituals. But I grew emboldened by the task before me and I did not let the old cove better me just to puff his gills.

"You saw him? Tell me, when?" my voice scolded. I watched him slit his eyes; the wetness of his moustaches drooped beyond the gobbet of his mouth like a drooling hound. I cut short his game and I saw he was not pleased.

"Now don't you take that tone with me, my boy," he said.

His voice was like a schoolmaster's – noisy and full of bluster – his design was to try and unhinge me. He wanted no less than to see me slink back from him like a whimpering pup that had just learned its first lesson at the end of a rolled newspaper. But I would not feed his desire; I had deeper passions aflame within me. I showed the old cove my back and kicked at the grey's flanks.

My family's hut in Mount Cameron's west was not so far on the back of a horse, but my mount did not warm to such a disrespectful handler as I galloped recklessly for home.

Great plumes of white breath came gushing from the grey's nostrils. The leather reins in my hands burned and cut blistered lines on my palms. For a second I feared the grey would drop upon the road. At a deep trench she seemed sure to collapse, but righted herself and I knew I must treat such obstacles with more care.

All the while my mind raced ever faster. My head was dizzy and I felt queasily unwell. Father was likely home already, perhaps even hunting my tiger to his death.

I knew that I'd allowed my father to steal home unopposed and now I could not rid myself of the thought that my tiger would soon pay.

Chapter Twenty-Eight

My mother fell into shock to see me home at such an hour, her tired breath greeting me in a hoarse blast. She reached for me with her hands outstretched; she sensed I was in an agitated condition. I clasped strongly at the hands she held out to me. "Mother where is he?"

"Myko, you're hurting me," she said, "let me go."

I looked down at my mother's thin hands; they were bony and veined from knuckle to wrist. "Tell me where he has gone. I need to know. Now!" I yelled.

My mother did not answer. She only stared into my eyes.

I let go of her hands and they fell lamely by her side; she quickly raised them and tucked them beneath her arms to build a barrier between us.

Tears welled in my mother's eyes as she spoke to me. "Myko, Myko, what is it? What has happened to you?" Over and over she pressed me, like the rush of a river pounding faster and faster, "Tell me, Myko, tell me, I am your mother … I am your mother."

I would not answer her; my mind was filled with panic and rage and I had no time to play the game of mother and dutiful son. I knew my father would not be upon the land so soon after his return without good reason; he was too tired to take on any tasks other than those of the utmost importance. Father would go out this day with one purpose alone – to hunt my tiger.

I stamped through our home with the same care I would give to the mud-holes of a swamp as I looked to find my father's hunting bag. I tumbled down a delicate shelf and tin plates fell loudly on the floor. The floorboards creaked sharp as log-splits beneath my heavy steps and the window's frame rattled in the wall as I pushed aside lanterns and dinner pots that stood in my way.

"Myko, what has become of you?" called out my mother, her face the image of sorrow, "why are you acting this way?"

"Father's hunting bag is gone," I said, pointing to the mess I had created in my search for the tools of his grim trade, "look, look … it's gone. Gone."

Mother moved towards me; "Myko, please, be at peace."

I turned away from her and walked towards our door. As I went, I saw a twist of strong hawser that usually hung on the door's back was missing.

"Myko, come back here!" shouted Mother.

I wanted to pay no attention to her but she was my mother and to hurt her this way wounded myself. I knew that I was taken with passions that I could not control, but I steeled myself to face her.

"Mother, I know what he is about. Don't try to hide it from me," I said.

As I watched her head drop before me I felt like my world was turning inside-out.

"Where did he go?" I said again. My voice sounded loud and strong, it echoed off the walls of our crude split-paling hut, and though I knew it distressed my mother, I would have raised it further and cried louder, if I were able.

"Where did he go?" I wailed.

"I do not know," said Mother; her hands now framed her face feebly, "he returned, and left again quickly."

"*To where?*"

My mind raced on, I knew of only one place he would be, but I did not want to believe it until I heard the words come from her lips. "Is he on a hunt?" I demanded.

Mother shrank from me and began to tremble with fear, her eyes darting back and forth as she cowered within her black shawl. I felt a dark impulse to grab her delicate shoulder blades and shake her where she stood, but I resisted, clutching again her thin-boned hands and squeezing them tightly.

"Myko, the dogs, they were wild with a tiger scent. He could not stay, he had to …" My mother's head dropped down on her chest. Her face was hidden as her words fell like vanished dreams. "It is his duty," she said, "he is sworn to his duty, he will not surrender his good name to anything else. Myko, you must know this, you must, you must understand, surely you must."

I placed my eyes upon my mother's grief-ravaged face and watched as she rubbed nervously at her neck-bones, but I had no words for her. I saw my father's actions had cut a scythe-sweep through her, as surely as they had done to me.

I ran from my mother and our home.

Anger drilled in my mind. I knew I must face my father and demand he leave my tiger to run free. I would not allow him to harm another beast to settle his bloodlust or greaten his hoard of weak praise and blandishments from Tasmania's bushmen and fools.

As I ran on the paddocks, grim imaginings chased my thoughts. The sky fell to a violet hue above a mountainous backdrop and allowed a narrow tongue of blood-red sun to seep onto the sea far beyond.

I saw the waters, green and still, touch the floury-white sands and I hoped my tiger had wandered far beyond his lair. I raced farther out across the button grasses and felt my feet touch the water-cut gullies that fed the silver streams.

The air held no sounds, save the limp cries of birdsong that I told my ears to ignore as I sought for tiger cries, and the baying of my father's dogs.

Branches cut at my face but I felt nothing as my eyes dug through the darkness of the forest. Black curls of crisp gnarled roots beneath the thin covering of soil struck like sabres as I stepped on them, but I did not slow my pace.

A gentle wind picked up and made a rushing sound through the branches that sounded like laughter following me. I quickened my steps to keep my track straight through the prying wind, but then I heard a piercing yap and I knew I must be upon my father's dogs.

The sounds fell far from my tiger's lair, outwith the forest and his hunting grounds. I ran as fast as I could against the gaining wind's unbroken gusts. The light fell hazily through the canopy, coming down in weak beams that struggled to light the way before me. The air burned hot and muffled the noise like fog as I broke into the open pastureland, and felt my blood run strangely cold.

The sky suddenly darkened above and dove-grey plumes of cloud fell all around me like heavy blankets of smoke. On top of the hill, where I stood, only the eucalypts saw farther afield. My eyes smarted in the new light; I felt them begin to water, and soon I found myself wiping at salty tears.

I saw my father had a wallaby tied in a lure. It was a small animal but a sprightly one and ran in desperate circles round its tether. He held the marsupial within a sheep pen, its hasty exertions kicking clouds of dust from the dry pasture beneath its beating leap.

My father hid beyond the pen, crouched in a shallow gorge; his rifle poked above his shoulder where he had it strapped to his back.

I felt my lips stiffen and knew at once my words were frozen in my throat. My legs felt heavy with fatigue and my breath fell into convulsions. Behind my long wandering gaze my mind numbed. I felt weak enough to be blown out like a candle in the breeze. I knew my tiger must be near.

My father understood his task full and well. He had trapped and snared many tigers. As this knowledge lanced into my heart

I felt sure I would soon see my tiger's end.

The wallaby's pounding suddenly increased within the pen. I would not have thought it likely, the poor creature looked near exhaustion, but it summoned further strength. I saw it gripped by terror as it completed frantic circles within what little distance it had to perform them. The creature's heart was ready to burst.

I had not witnessed a more desperate scene. I felt for the poor beast's fate, its eyes were etched with panic. And then, as if attached to a length of fishing line, my tiger was pulled from the scrub upon the pen, and quickly clutched the wallaby within his widened jaws, bringing it down with one fell swoop.

The wallaby suffered little. I believe it met its end with great speed, but I could not watch what followed.

"No. No. No," I called out.

I knew my tiger's fate was sealed. He had taken the bait laid by my father and now my slim hope of finding his freedom was gone.

When I unfurled my tight-closed eyes I watched my father run to close the pen behind my tiger. I saw Father turn himself quickly to one side, his eyes suddenly probing further afield as he side-stepped awkwardly and roared to his pack of dogs. I could not see what he pointed at but I knew it must be my tiger's mate.

Quickly, I ran for my father. The distance seemed great from the hill-top to the goings below. I watched Father run, too; as he went he unfurled a burlap sack from beneath his coat and then he scooped up two tiger cubs and fastened upon a third.

All drowsiness left my blood as I cut the air to where my father rested in peaceful conquest. I ran faster and faster and I soon came close enough to hear him greet me. "*Myko, Myko,*" he called.

I did not respond. I ran straight for the sheep pen to where he held his quarry.

"Myko, what is wrong?" said Father.

A heavy scent clung in the air as my father stood smoothing his whiskers before the tiger, which devoured its prey in the sheep pen.

I felt ready to grasp the gun from my father's hand should he prepare to fire on my tiger. I watched him with cautious eyes; I dared not remove my gaze. "What will you do with it?" I demanded.

As he turned to face me I sensed my presence was no more surprise to him than a tide touching a sandbar. "That is quite a greeting, Myko. Hello, my son," he said, and then he turned away once more.

"The tiger, Father, do not kill it!" I was bleary-eyed but my voice held strong.

He began to unfurl his rifle before me. "They are a pest, my son."

My thoughts drifted in and out. I twitched nervously as I thought to snatch the rifle from him. "Do not kill it! I warn you."

My father drew his stare back to me, his eyes narrowed as he took me in. I knew he sized me for my actions; he tried to judge the strength of my determination.

"Myko, the tigers are a threat to the flocks," he said slowly.

"Do not kill it," I said. My teeth were gritted, my jaws clasped tight. I could see the gun in his hand; I watched him pull pack the hammer and I was ready to take it from him. I was ready to fight with my own father and the thought drew shame into me.

"Myko!" he said, shocked. As he walked towards me I could see I had displeased him more than ever I had.

Chapter Twenty-Nine

When my father came back to us in the Sakiai, we believed ourselves blessed by God above.

Father looked pale and weak, his skin tawny around his mouth and eyes. I saw marks on his face that were not there before. One of the marks, a hard dark scar above his chin, ran under his jawline and back towards his ear. This jagged, tormenting battle wound made me unhappy; I did not like to think of my father having suffered with the pain it must have caused him.

"I have eaten nothing for three days bar fish heads begged from guardsmen on the train," said Father; he had little strength, his journey had tired him out.

"Where did you come from?" my brother asked, the happiness in his voice a joy to hear.

"I came from an army camp," said Father, "six hundred miles south-east of Moscow." As he spoke he kept a steady eye on his wife his gaze drew out my own. When I turned to my mother I felt shocked to see her trapped behind a veil of terror, her face black as tarpaper.

As I watched my mother she shifted nervously, it seemed as though the boards beneath her feet burned too hot for her to stand. Her left eyelid carried a tic and her delicate fingers rubbed endlessly on the two white triangles of her lace dress-collars.

In time my mother calmed.

There came not a single day following Father's return that we did not bless the Lord and give up our thanks. My mother shone, in ways we had not seen before.

"Drink up, drink up, you need to build your strength," Mother said as she nursed our father, feeding him broth and onions cooked in goat's milk.

"Daina, you are my strength," said Father. He pulled my mother onto his knee and stroked her long black hair, held in pretty braids, piled high on her head.

My mother laughed like a girl and my father smiled widely; but I knew the strangers in our home did not share my parents' joys.

Pranciskis viewed these goings through slitted eyes. He flopped sulkily in front of the fireside and sucked in his pockmarked cheeks as he drew tapers to light his pipes.

"Are there no chores to be done around the farm?" he said, "Or are we all to spend the day giggling like children?"

Pranciskis sat forward with his nose pinched to the flames, his earlobes burning red, and his eyes sewn tightly closed. He looked to all the world like a fencepost blown cockeyed after a storm. Deep currents raged within him. I knew Pranciskis planned something for us; it seemed like he waited for his moment to show us that he was still our better.

In time my mother lost the sparkle of youth which had lit her since Father's return and went back to her weeping ways.

"I cannot take this," she burst out one morning.

My father let out a great sigh; I wondered if it was heard around the whole house.

"Daina ..." he said, drawing my mother to him.

"No, it is no good, Petras," she pushed him away, "it is no good."

My mother ran from him. As we watched her climbing the staircase we grew quickly anxious. We knew a change was coming with the wind. We lived inside a tinderbox, like little pieces of touchwood, awaiting one spark to send us all into flames.

"Daina," my father called as he ran at her back.

Jurgis followed to my parents' bedroom door, but I held

him before he rushed in. Through a gap of some inches below the door we watched my mother crying. She sat on the edge of the bed with her soft, frail neck lowered, her head held in her hands, her long black hair hanging lamely before her.

My father stepped around her; he drew his hands in fists, his strides were full of purpose. "Why, but why would he do it?" His face looked to be mixed with worry and confusion.

My mother did not reply to Father's question, she merely continued sobbing from behind her tangled mass of hair and cupped her hands over her face.

"But I have not quarrelled with him," said Father, his voice strained, his words clipped in tone. "Even though he is living below my roof!"

I watched my mother roll on her side. I saw her shaking where she lay as she called out my father's name. "Petras, Petras, please understand, I know him, I know him too well."

Mother's sobs deepened to animal wails, wild cries of despair that she made no attempt to disguise. I saw her press her fingers into her eye-sockets and I wondered if she tried to force back her tears. She had drawn the last drop and dreg of her strength.

My father went to her side again. He placed a hand on her back and then he took a piece of paper from her grasp and looked at it for a moment.

My mother sat up abruptly. "Give me that!" She snatched back the paper and tore it into shreds. "Let the Czar go to hell!" she cried, "Let the Czar go to hell!"

My mother's teeth gritted as she tore at the paper and cast it into tiny pieces. Madness filled her eyes. I had never seen my mother act this way before.

"The army returned you to me," she said, "to me, the army returned you to me!"

Mother fell upon the bed, weeping. Her face lay hidden

from me and from my father, who watched her where she lay, his hand outstretched, but not daring to touch her.

The sun shone fuller through the windows and yellow blades of light lowered down upon my mother and father. I was close enough to see the dust play in the light's glow but I did not understand anything of the scene before me.

"No, Daina," said Father, "the army had no idea where I was. Until someone told them."

My father paused. "Now, they will come for me."

Mother sat upright; tears ran upon her face and more welled in her eyes. "I will not lose you again," she said. As she spoke I sensed the brute anger in her voice. "I will not."

Father held Mother close to him, and a finger of sunlight drew a line between his heavy shoulders. Above my mother's heartfelt cries I could just make out my father's words: "Then what choice do we have, Daina, *what* choice?"

Early the next morning, before Pranciskis and the others had risen, my family fled from our home.

We crossed the holding yard first, and then the green fields. We walked silently for a long time. Mother and Father kept especially quiet, passing few words between them.

As I listened to the birds singing their sweet tunes of the early morning, the entire countryside lay completely still. We followed the morning's mist as it retreated over the hillside and watched the sun rise higher in the sky, so high that it soon sat upon the white clouds, which stole all the warmth of the sun's rays and darkened the path before us.

Suddenly everything changed. After miles and miles of walking peacefully on the road, the air around us quickly filled with an unearthly disquiet.

"What is that noise, Myko?" asked my brother.

I had no answer for him. "Stop and listen," I said, "we might hear it better then."

The noise began like a siren, slowly being wound by hand, building all around us. It came from behind us, beyond the hill, where a violent sky had spread.

"Petras, I am scared," said Mother.

My father halted in the road and looked back. Together we tried to place the source of the discord. As we stood, the noise grew and then, as we waited in fear, all was revealed to us.

Pranciskis came into view. He rode on his bicycle, the one which Kazimeras fashioned for him by removing one of the pedals and attaching a thick wooden block for his withered limb to rest upon.

He screamed down at us. "Wait, wait, Daina you must wait," he roared from the pits of his lungs.

As he called out Mother's name his face turned dark as a beet. "Wait, wait, Daina … Wait where you are!" he roared.

As the wheels upon his bicycle turned at great speed, he spat these words out again and again: "Wait, Daina, wait!" He seemed full of purpose as he descended on us, his coat-tails flying in the wind that met him as he gathered pace.

I watched Pranciskis's face become darker. The wind forced creases on his brow and cut black folds into the hollows below his eyes; I noticed he waved a pistol in his hand.

"Wait where you are!" he roared.

He tried to steady his course as he pointed the pistol towards us, roaring all the while, "Wait, I say. Wait."

I turned to Father but he did not acknowledge me. He merely continued to gaze at Pranciskis high on the hill, descending towards us at great speed.

I called out, "Father, Father," but he remained motionless and then I felt a torrent of fear strike as a gunshot split the air.

"*Father*," I yelled.

As I looked towards the hill, I saw Pranciskis falling from his bicycle. His arms flailed wildly as he met the road's curve and then I watched him come to rest, and lie face down in a heap on the ground.

Not a twitch came from him as I heard his bicycle overturn on the dark, hard road. I looked away and saw the bicycle's back wheel spinning violently; it continued in hasty revolution until it lost momentum and its turn slowed down to the slightest of ticks.

From beyond a stone wall stepped Karolis, the village smuggler. He wore a rifle slung on his back. My father held out his hand to him; "God blessed, be praised," he said.

Karolis stepped forward but did not take Father's hand. "You have something for me?" he said curtly.

Father unbuttoned his shirt and removed a paper package filled with money, which he handed over to Karolis. As he peered into the package Karolis's eyes darted first on my father, and then all around us.

"I must count," he said.

It took Karolis some time to count the money.

I knew Karolis was once a *Knygnesys*, a book smuggler. I remembered seeing him at our home once, before the soldiers took away our father, long before the others came.

"Hurry, get the cripple out of sight," said Karolis.

My father raised Pranciskis and carried him on his back towards the roadside. After a few steps Father lowered the lifeless body over a stony wall at the edge of a field.

I followed the goings-on keenly. Where Pranciskis lay I stared down and saw his blood-splattered face and neck. His hair lay torn clean away on one side; his skull beneath looked as smooth as the head on an old coin.

"We have no time to spare," said Karolis, "this hold up has robbed us of more time than we can afford. Come, we must move quickly."

We left the road hurriedly, setting out upon the fields.

Karolis and my parents took large strides and my brother and I ran to keep up. I looked down to my brother and encouraged him to speed up. "Come on Jurgis, you are falling behind," I said, but he did not respond to me. My brother's head was bowed, his spindly legs moving quickly to keep up with the others.

The fields were wet. We brought great splashes up from the ground with every step and soon we were soaked through with mud.

I looked again at my brother, he seemed tired, his face white as he drew deep breaths with his every stride.

"Jurgis, we must try harder to stay together," I said.

"It is as fast as I can go, Myko."

I reached out to him, I had no choice but to drag him along. "Here, give me your hand."

Soon we arrived by a railway track. The train halted for a few brief seconds and Karolis spoke quickly to my father. "The train stops before the border. You must follow the instructions carefully; only one Russian guard has been paid and he will leave his post for but a brief moment – you must be ready then, you will have little time. Is this clear?"

My father nodded. "It is clear."

"Then good luck. And may God be with you," said Karolis, as we left him behind and quickly ran to clamber on board the train.

In our damp carriage, my brother dropped to the floor and began to cry. I watched him shiver where he lay, face down in the scattering of dirty straw. We travelled in a cattle mover, horded with many beasts; we could taste the stench of their confinement.

"Son, do not cry," my father told Jurgis, "there will be many new things for you to see. We will soon be in a far better place, where we can all start again. I promise it will be a better place, I promise you, my boy."

As my father stroked at Jurgis's head I moved to sit by his side. "Where, Papa?" I asked, "where is the better place?"

Father's face opened into a wide smile and his voice boomed, "We are going to America, my boys," he said, "what an adventure we will have there!"

I did not know the word. He said it again and I repeated it slowly; "*AM-ER-ICA*."

"That is it," said Father, "you see, you have it already."

The noise from the carriage's shudders disturbed the cattle and some of them released their water. My brother began to cry again, but Father raised himself to stand, peering over the stalls and above the backs of the cattle towards the landscape.

I knew my father took one last look at his homeland. I saw his face becoming grim and wan. His dark whiskers seemed to droop lower than before, as if they too worried, and burrowed further down his face. As I turned from him I saw my mother now faced the opposite way, staring blankly toward the cattle. I wondered what she thought of, but I knew better than to disturb her when she was this way.

After a long time in the carriage, two loud jolts threw us about, and then we heard the screeching noise of metal upon metal.

"That is the brakes," said Father, "don't worry about that noise … it means we have arrived."

I looked out and saw our carriage come to a halt, but we stopped far from the station, and farther still from the border.

"Quick, we must get off here," said Father.

I watched Mother – who had sat silently alone throughout the journey – rush to raise Jurgis to her, but suddenly, where she stood, she let her hands fall to her side. My mother let go of her handkerchief and the wind came in to take it away. I watched the little handkerchief carried high up in the air and then float away like a little yellow bird. But my mother did not seem to care.

"What is it?" said Father, crouching beside Mother and Jurgis.

"He has a fever."

My father looked at Jurgis and then swiftly raised him aloft, holding him closely beneath the broad nap of his heavy coat. "We have a long way to go; come, we must move quickly."

Chapter Thirty

"Myko," said Father; his voice came calmly, his words carrying less weight than the air, "I will not kill the tiger, but I will not have it upon this land."

I knew my father to be no liar. If he said he would spare my tiger then I accepted this as his word. My normal breath returned and I removed my eyes from him; I felt too much shame to face him now.

For the first time since I had been on top of the hill I was free to gaze upon my tiger, but, as I turned towards the corral my heart missed a beat – it was not him.

The tiger was a female, she looked small and very young. She held fewer stripes upon her back than my tiger and, from hunger, ribs poked beneath her fur.

"It's a young slut," said Father, "she has ranged far." I felt his gaze sear into me. "Myko, did you know about this tiger on our land?"

"No, Father," I said, "I have not seen this tiger before." I knew I spoke not one word of a lie.

The tiger sat motionless as a statue where my father trapped her in a rough cage made from fencing wood. She appeared to be most docile and offered little resistance; if it wasn't for the presence of her cubs I believe the tiger may have expired from fright.

"What is wrong with her?" I asked my father, "why does she not fight?"

Father tested the latch upon the cage, it held fast.

"It is not a dog, Myko," said Father, "this is the tiger's way. A snared dog will fight his trappers, but not a tiger."

I thought it natural for an animal to fight against a trapper, but with tigers, I saw it was different. My father ripped open a sack and threw it over the cage, the tiger seemed unmoved.

"The dog packs which roam the station fight so hard they choke to death," I said.

"Their trappers should shoot them before that happens," said Father.

I knew the tiger was smarter than any dog. "Maybe the tiger knows there is no point in struggling."

My father stood up straight, and kicked at the tiger's cage; "Maybe all tigers are cowards, Myko, did you ever think of that?" he said.

I knew this to be untrue. "No. They are not!"

Father walked before me and placed his hands on his hips, then spoke firmly; "I have seen tigers simply wilt and die in a snare; they just give up. Or, after placing a single hand on them, they collapse with fright … that is a fact, Myko."

I knew the tiger to be a tender animal, but to trappers like my father this marked it as a coward. My father saw no value in such a sensitive creature, save the money he earned from its pelt. But I knew the truth. I had seen my own tiger's brave fight.

"The tiger is no coward," I said.

"I have gathered up tigers as easily as lambs, Myko. I know these animals."

Father tore open another sack and placed it over the cage, the tiger stirred this time, but very little. I knew my father had not killed this female tiger or her cubs because they had become so rare, but because they held a higher price alive.

"What will you do with them?" I asked him.

"They will go to Hobart," said Father.

"To the zoo?"

My father's eyes wandered over the caged beasts and then he pitched himself forward and his mouth jerked into a grin. "They will pay twelve pounds for the tiger," he said, "these useless creatures are worth more now alive than when they were a plague and we had the bounty!"

I saw he felt pleased with his haul.

"And the cubs?"

Father filled his cheeks and let out his breath slowly before he spoke again. "... And ten, yes, I think ten shillings for each pup."

As my father secured the cage he looked up to the sky. "There is time left in the day," he said.

"Time left for what?" I asked.

I watched for an answer and saw him crease his eyes to the sky once more. His skin grew weathered by the sun, it was tight-lined and deeply-rutted. Dark shadows sat under his eyes and in the hollows of his face as his pallor took on the colour of dead leaves.

"Time left for what?" I asked again.

Father lowered his gaze to me, "I have time to take the haul to the carter in Woolnorth, he will be leaving for Hobart today."

I knew these tigers had taken their last breath of freedom.

"He will charge me, of course," said Father, "but there will be plenty in the payment to come."

As Father spoke I felt a deep desolation sink into my heart. I wanted to take the tiger and her cubs from him, but I could not see how.

The light picked up the purple hue above the hills and I moved away from my father to return to the pastures. As I went I did not alert him to my departure; I found it too hard to form the words to address him now, least not without shovelling hatred at him.

I took back on the woods; it fell dark beneath the trees. The few breaks in the canopy above looked like stars in the night sky. I travelled slowly, feeling for the roots and vines as I went, but I did not worry about becoming lost in the blackening forest, because my thoughts were far away.

The billabongs glistened like crystals as I pushed through the vaults of branches. My heels felt heavy as I went but no matter how hard I pressed my steps, or put distance between myself and my father, I could not escape the thoughts that came to me from out of the dark shadows.

I wandered far into the forest. Night fell and I wandered farther still. I followed only a sharp desire to rid myself of what I had seen, but I could not.

Soon I came upon the station at Woolnorth; I tried to pick out the billet's window where Tilly slept beyond. I gathered up pebbles and gently cast them onto the window's ledge. The pebbles clipped the ledge and bounced on the glass and the noise scraped and scratched like possums in the night. It did not take long to attract Tilly's attention.

"Who is there?" she whispered into the darkness.

"It's me – Myko."

"Myko," said Tilly, "what are you doing here?"

"Come out here, come out now. I have something to tell you."

Tilly opened wide the window. The rusty clasp fastener screeched like a plough's blade on a rock as she held the frame steadily for a moment. When the window was widened no more noise came and soon I heard only Tilly's footsteps churning up the dry earth.

"Myko, where have you been? They have been looking for the grey mare." "She is at my home. I took her to stop my father."

Tilly lowered her head. "I didn't want to tell you about the hunt, Myko." She quickly lifted her eyes to my face. "I knew you would be angry."

"Tilly, I am not angry," I said, "not with you."

Tilly smiled at me. "I am glad."

We walked out into the night; away from the billet the air came sharp with the wood's rich tang. At the water trough we sat on the ground and laid our backs against the cold, damp iron. I saw Tilly's face clearly under the moon's light.

"She had lost her mate," I said.

"*What* – who has?"

"The tiger. The tiger my father trapped."

"He caught a tiger?"

"Yes, he trapped her with a wallaby tied in a lure."

Tilly raised up her hands and buried her face in her palms; as she spoke her words fell like whispers. "Did he kill the tiger?"

"No. It was a female with cubs … he will sell them in Hobart."

Tilly drew back her hands and showed her face to me. "Then at least they are still alive, Myko. That is something, that he didn't kill them."

I said nothing, I thought of the tiger's pitiful journey, and how it ended in such misery. I believed the tiger my father caught must have lost her mate; perhaps she followed my own tiger's scent in the hope of winning his protection for her cubs.

"She had ranged a great distance and she was half-starved and very weak," I said.

"She came to the wrong place," said Tilly.

I knew the tiger's senses taught her to seek out her own kind, and this was the distance she had had to cross to find another. "You are right," I said, "this is the wrong place."

"The wrong place for any tiger."

I stood up quickly, I felt the blood suddenly come rushing in my head. "You are right, Tilly," I said, "you are right!"

As I ran back towards the road, to the trees beyond, my mind was spinning; I had to find my tiger. I had to move him on, before my father found him.

"Myko, where are you going?" called Tilly as I went.

The road behind me was a blur as I called back to her, "I must go, Tilly. I have to go."

"Myko, Myko … where are you going?"

I ran harder and stretched out my paces as I crossed the station tracks, and made the pasture quickly. Tilly and the billet fell into the distance as I ran on. She's right, this is the wrong place for any tiger, I thought as I ran on.

Soon I grew tired and I wandered in the dark forest for a long time. I had no idea of where I found myself as tough strands of tanglefoot pulled at my ankles and damp branches drooled on my face.

The forest grew cold and gave over its silence to the hum of insects that flitted under the white flashes of moonlight that appeared like ghosts from above. My shirtsleeves grew wet and ragged as I forced my way through the thick undergrowth.

I felt exhausted, and lost. I slumped against a tree and my lungs began to rise and fall as I gasped for air. I dropped, defeated, to the ground, and then to my amazement, I heard a movement behind me. "Now will you let me help?" said a soft voice.

As I turned, I saw Tilly. "*You* – you followed me all the while."

Chapter Thirty-One

A flock of lorikeets fled screaming for the skies as the creek cried over the rocks in the night-time. The white moon shone brightly when Tilly's voice broke the forest's silence, but my breathing became hard as I stared on at her. I could not believe my eyes.

"You followed me!" I said.

"I want to help you, Myko."

I threw up my hands; "I don't need your help … you shouldn't have come here."

"Myko, you are lost. It looks to me like you need my help."

As I gazed about me, raindrops began to fall, driving tiny pin-pricks in my flesh. The air felt sharp and cold.

"I am not lost … I am not."

"Myko, why won't you let me help? What is it you are hiding?"

A hollow cry leapt within me; I knew that I couldn't say what I was hiding.

"Myko, please let me help you. I am your friend." As Tilly spoke I felt my pulse quicken. I turned and ran from her, straight into the dark woods.

The forest was a hive of activity, nocturnal animals let out hoots and calls. Hanging branches and stringybark scratched at my face and hands, and underfoot I trampled over cone bushes and sweet scented buttercups alike. I had no respect for the island, everything was in my way.

"Myko, come back," I heard Tilly call.

I ran on, nearly crushing a blue-tongued skink beneath my foot. It hissed at me and brought me close to a fall, but I did not stop to offer a reply to the wag of its jaws.

"Myko, Myko," Tilly continued to call out.

She kept pace with me as I trampled over bracken and the clay-baked footpaths. My brows grew heavy and my knees weakened; I knew that I could not escape her.

I stopped running and lowered myself down onto a humpbacked rock. A mob of blowflies settled on me at once and made tormenting dives on my eyes and mouth.

As Tilly came back into sight she smiled, and then she took a few steps closer. "You can't get away, Myko."

I felt myself smiling back at her. "I think you're right," I said, "what's the point in running from you?"

Tilly moved to join me on the rock, where she sat at my side. I felt her breath as heavy as my own after our run through the forest. My face grew wet with sweat and my limbs ached and twitched as I felt the night's breeze on my cheek, and the bitter citrus smell of the forest come to my nostrils.

"Why are you here, Myko?" said Tilly, her voice low and soft.

"The tigers," I said.

"I knew it must be. But the tigers are gone now, Myko, your father trapped them, you said so yourself."

I thought of the female tiger and her cubs that my father had trapped – they were on their way to Hobart now. I knew my father would soon have his blood money; at once I saw his face rise in my mind.

"No, Tilly." I stood before her. "There is another tiger."

Tilly's mouth fell open; I believe she struggled for words. I knew she feared that there would be trouble brought with this new knowledge.

I raised my voice. "Tilly," I said, "you cannot tell anyone!"

She jumped up and faced me at no more than an inch away. "Myko, how could you think that I ever would?"

"Tilly, my father, he …"

"Myko, your father is the station's tiger man. His pride

will be hurt if he finds out. How have you kept it from him until now?"

"I didn't; the other tiger, the female, she strayed onto my tiger's lands and Father's dogs sought her out. Tilly, I must find my tiger – he has a mate and cubs."

"That is what you are doing, Myko, looking for this tiger?"

"Yes, but I can't find him. There may have been trouble with the other tiger, which drove him away already, and the trapping, the dogs may have spooked him."

"But how will you find a tiger, Myko?"

"If I don't find him my father will … Tilly, my father will know I deceived him, that I kept my tiger from him. He will be angry. I will be punished and the greatest punishment he could give me is to kill my tiger."

Tilly turned away from me; she faced a dark path through the forest. "This way, Myko," she called out.

"Why that way?"

"Come on," roared Tilly as she set off from me, "we will find your tiger."

Tilly sent me running once more, scouring the low forests which butted our home pastures. As I moved, with heavy, plodding strides, my skin became flayed by sharp branches that lashed out like stock whips. Twigs and fallen bark-strips were caught up with moss balls that blew on the forest tracks, scampering in every direction like lines of busy ants.

We ranged on for hours in the dark of the forest, until I found myself returned close to a familiar point. The sky above was moonless and beneath the branches' shadows a crisp light flooded in with the new day.

"Tilly, hold up," I said.

"What is it? Have you seen something?"

"I know this place."

I stared into what looked like a small cave, with a floor of clay and earth. It was hollowed out and lined with twigs and grass. I could just make out the tiny scratchings on the lair's edge, outside and in, where the newborn cubs had scrambled with their tiny claws.

"What, what is it?" said Tilly.

"This is my tiger's lair. Look – there are wildfowl bones, my tiger must have brought them back to feed the cubs."

I stood at the lair knowing my tiger had been here, but I could not say when. I feared for him now, and for his family. I imagined their slow trail through the forest in search of sanctuary, once again. Why must they be hounded like this? I thought.

"Myko, he has gone. The lair is empty."

I ran into the scrub and turned up the thickets and fallen branch stems. I kicked at the tall grasses and gazed into the sun-baked wastes and flat reed beds.

"Myko, the tiger is gone," said Tilly again.

"I need to know he is safe – that he's far from this place."

Tilly came to my side and placed her hand upon the arm I thrashed at the grasses with; I could find no sign of him.

"Myko, you must stop now. We have looked all night. The tiger is gone; we must go back home, we will be missed if we don't."

I didn't want to listen to her. "You go back, Tilly," I said.

"Myko, come with me."

"No, Tilly. I will stay and look for my tiger. You go back."

Tilly turned away from me and I felt her lower the hand she held on my arm. "Goodbye, Myko," she said, "I hope you find him."

I did not trust my tiger's safety to fate. I knew I must keep to my search. I thrashed in the scrub, the sun came up high and hot, moisture rose on my back while I roamed in the high grasses.

191

I trailed across the smooth-pebbled beaches and the shore flats above the bays. I trudged in the tumbledown whiteness of the high wattle grasses and I scoured beneath the misty blue hills. For many hours I searched, but I saw nothing of my tiger. As the poor animal's chances played out in my imagination I began to feel my emotions give way to panic.

My steps slowed as another day's light began to fade, and darkness drew down on me. Though the stars seemed close I stumbled many times and through my tired eyes I could not see where to place my feet before me.

I lost all hope of finding my tiger. As I waved my defeat to the wind and trees, I fell backwards into a thicket of silver bracken.

I had failed my tiger; where he was, or where even I had wandered, I did not know.

I felt ready to weep; I rolled onto my knees and looked up to the dark sky, but it held no answers for me. I threw back my head and let my limbs fold beneath me. A hard tree-bole scratched at my back, ripping my shirt and stabbing at me as I fell. And then, where I came to rest, two bright yellow eyes lit up.

My tiger had found me.

Chapter Thirty-Two

I reached out and there was no fear in my tiger's eyes. I felt the trees above hang around us in deep curiosity as my breathing stopped.

I crouched down on the age-soft stones as the high clouds broke and burnished us together in the moon's light. I fell in a trance, looking at my tiger as the mist clung to the night's air and carried off my thoughts.

My tiger's dun-coloured coat shone as I neared him. He did not seem to mind how close I came, he merely stared on at me with round, wet eyes that seemed buried deep in the forest.

I felt my heart pulse and glow with pride. I was lost in a dream to be with my tiger, and then, suddenly, the surrounding darkness flooded in on us and at once I sank powerless in a blur of emotion.

As I gazed at the dampness of my tiger's fur I saw blood. There was a wound beneath his ear; he was hurt. I drew nearer to look him over fully, and saw his coat streamed wet with blood, the flesh beneath ripped and torn.

Thoughts spun in my head. My tiger's wounds were raw and fresh; I knew he had been set upon by dogs.

"Who has done this to you?" I whispered.

Few dogs will turn on a tiger, even when in packs they fear tigers greatly. Alone, a very large dog, a roo dog or a shepherd's hound, would not go against a tiger. Dogs must be trained for such a task, like my father's.

"Has he found you?" I said softly.

I saw now that my tiger panted, his breath came white against the darkness. I tried to encourage him to rest, but he was too alert, raking his claws in the rotten branches and fallen bark upon the forest floor.

He stood on his hinds like a straight-grown tree. Were my tiger a dog he would have barked frantically to capture my attention – but he was a tiger – he made no noise save the yappings he spared for his mate, within their hunt. Softly, he nuzzled his snout beneath my arm as if to raise me.

"What, what is it?" I said. I stood up and my tiger, I believe, turned to draw me.

Angles of moonlight showed the dark blood-patches on his coat. As he ran, his back-legs caught on an uneven bank and I saw he was part-lame, and in pain. I took his lead and followed after my tiger, through the bush once more.

As I felt my way the sky cleared above us and the moon, removed of cloud, shone down upon the forest. I saw clearly the severity of my tiger's wounds now. He had fought bravely against many dogs and I knew he must soon be brought down by his injuries and his exhaustion. But my tiger's steps were strong; he held a mighty force within his animal heart.

Respect deepened within me for my tiger's fight. He had little left to give to his battle yet he did not allow himself to falter. I saw that my tiger was far braver than any man. What pains he suffers, I thought. And yet he did not let them draw him from his purpose.

As my tiger pressed hard into the bush, his nose following a silent trail, his steps fell ungainly, his tail so long and straight it made him turn all about like a boat in the sea. He possessed none of the agility of other animals, my tiger's movements were his alone.

Anger kindled the hurts inside me as I ran through a slough of high reeds by the rapid singing stream. I followed the strong musky scent of my tiger as he cut his way through the heavily wooded patches. I crashed through twigs and stringy branches that whipped against me with stinging pain, but I felt nothing. I was a streak of rage as I thundered through the forest.

The mist rose and the waters grew faster, as fast as the blood pumping in my ears. The pace of my tiger also grew; he ran high in his stride, his narrow hips pushing him on through the coarse country. I did not understand this need to quicken his steps, and then all of a sudden, I heard dogs barking in the distance.

"Wait, wait," I called out to my tiger, "wait there!"

I watched my tiger's pace quicken yet again, we headed straight to the dogs. I understood he ran towards his end, and it made me stop still with fright.

"Wait, wait!" I tried to call back my tiger again, but he was gone from me, racing fast through the covering of man ferns.

The dogs grew nearer; their barking seemed only a few feet away as I raced after my tiger. I did not know what I would find there, but as I went I gathered up a fallen branch from a red gum. I felt its girth; its contours were strong. I intended to yield it like a waddy and fight alongside my tiger.

I will fight to the end if I must, I told myself.

We reached a clearing, a natural spot where trees had fallen in the forest, and yet, a fire burned strongly here. It had been burning for some time, sending pewter-coloured smoke spirals to the stars. The high amber flickers of the flame lit the trunks and branches and sent giant moths dancing in the open, where wattle bats swooped on them, grateful for their easy taking.

I knew my tiger's appearance at this open clearing was not unexpected, this arena was carefully chosen. As I stepped from the bush behind my tiger I saw who had brought us here – it was my father.

Waves of hate and emotion crashed over me; my mind swam feebly as I stared at my father and his baying dogs.

"You!" I called as a drawn-out blade of light fell on my father's face. I spied the whitened lines of scars that followed his jawline down into his collars.

"No, Father! No. No." I pleaded with him, my hands raised like a surrender.

My father portrayed no emotion, his features held as firm as a tight-nailed slab of board. His eyes lacked any life as they locked on my tiger as tight as iron-shackles.

"Step out of the way, Myko. Now!" he roared.

Below his grasp, father's dogs charged with all hell's fury, their jaws attacking the air with bites. Though he stood as broad as a swamp gum, my father struggled hard to hold the angry mob of dogs; they tested even his strength and in little time Father was forced to loose some of the pack from his grasp.

The hounds reached for my tiger; three at once, they ran for him. I watched my tiger raise himself on his hinds and open wide his jaws; they were twice the gape of any dog.

The first dog my tiger caught was Father's heeler dog; he cleared off half its head with one great bite. The dog fell before us; his skull was exposed and the red of his arteries spilled, it seemed, all at once.

The other dogs were smaller and did not envy their leader's fate. I watched them run whimpering from the clearing, their ears flat, their tails bowed low beneath them.

Where my tiger stood square upon the ground he had won, he faced towards my father; I too fell into my father's full view, but he would not look at me. He was ashamed of me. I had let him down.

"No, Father. No more."

"You should have told me, Myko," he said.

I had earned his outrage, but I knew I could never have told him of any tiger on his holding.

My eyes took in my father's grimacing face. "You should have been truthful," he said, "these tigers are a pest."

"They are not!" I yelled at him.

"They are a threat to the flocks, Myko. It is my duty to hunt them."

"They are not a threat, they are nearly wiped out. How can they be a threat? You are wrong, you are wrong to hunt them. I hate what you have done!"

His face seemed pained and drawn. I could not have hurt him more had I thrown his heart upon the ground, stamped on it soundly, and pressed it underfoot.

I did not wish to challenge my father in this way or any other. He was the man who had raised me. What mettle I had within me was the same as ran inside his veins, but the line was drawn in the dirt, and now it was time for one of us to pass.

"Get out of the way, Myko," he said.

My father aimed to teach me of my wrongdoing. I knew his lesson would be a harsh one; I saw that as clear as the white moon moving above us.

"I said move, Myko!"

Father's eyes moved slowly on my tiger.

"No!" I said. "You cannot kill my tiger. I won't allow you."

Had I been a willing son then I would have stepped aside. I would have learnt his lesson, become simply the tin pail he kicked to test, but I could not betray my tiger.

Wild thoughts coursed like thornfish through my emotions. I had my reserves of rage, but I felt fatigued and worn. I was lost to myself as surely as ever I had been.

"Step aside, Myko," said my father; his voice was calm but firm and I sensed the force it held.

I gripped tightly on the waddy. "I won't. You will not take my tiger," I said.

As my father took a step towards me I could no more judge the right course than a blind man could latch hands on a feral cat. I gripped again on the waddy and resolved to leave my actions to God.

Chapter Thirty-Three

My mother sobbed as my family stepped down from the train leaving the Sakiai, but if my father felt any worries he did not show them. As all our eyes turned to him, where he carried Jurgis, he hastened his stride. "Come quickly, we will be best to move along as fast as we can."

What faced us through the failing light was like a picture I had drawn many times. I imagined the scene before us to be a birthday cake. A huge cake, it might have been either round or square for I could not see its edges, it was so vast.

Down the cake's centre I saw the birthday candles placed, in two neat rows. These candles marked a boundary – the high fences of wire. At the cake's top, where the candles flamed, barbed wire curled in great round bunches.

I saw that the cake was cut, but not in a neat wedge. This slice went right down the middle, searing the cake in two. On each half burned candles, and at either side down its great missing cleft, they burned there too.

The picture filled my imagination; I thought that it could not be true, who makes a cake like this? But it is what I saw, as I stood in the snow, watching the searchlight make the birthday cake and its candles sparkle for as far as my eyes could see.

"We must walk around the ditch," said Father, his voice raking the air, "it cannot go on forever."

I stared into the ditch and wondered how such a gorge could have been cut out; was it by a huge plough? Was it a line of prisoners, a gang in chains, perhaps? I did not know.

Father spoke again and the picture slowly vanished. "Come on, follow me where I go. The ditch cannot go on forever, it cannot."

My mother stared ahead, blank-eyed. Dark shadows

loomed beneath her open mouth, which blew out a high airy voice; "How can you say?" she said. Mother did not seem convinced, she stared unbelieving at my father as he shifted my brother like a sack's weight.

"We will find its end, it must end somewhere," said Father, "and then we will follow it back to where we must go; you must trust me Daina."

Mother sighed again, and said under her breath, "What choice do we have?"

Jurgis kept quiet beneath the close weave of Father's coat as we set off in the darkness once more. The glow of the station and the great arc of the searchlight traced the boundary for us as we went. But soon our path grew dim, and eventually the heavy darkness surrounded us. All around fell a blackness. As I held my hand out, to barely beyond my nose, I could not see it.

We crawled slowly on and my mother and father took turns carrying Jurgis. "I want to walk by myself," said my brother, as he struggled in my mother's arms.

"Jurgis, you have a fever. You cannot walk by yourself," she scolded him.

"I can. I can. Let me go," he said.

My brother struggled on and Father stretched out a hand to rest on Jurgis's brow. "He is cooler now," he said, "let the boy walk if he wants to, Daina."

Mother grew worried as we continued through the night. "Sound out your names, boys. So I know where you are," she said.

"I am here," my brother's voice came weakly, but his pebble-round eyes shone bright as he followed close to my steps.

We were all very tired; in the darkness we seemed to have walked a great distance and I could no longer tell if the boundary existed. I felt the wire of the fence, I touched it to guide my way along its cold edge, but I did not see the ditch. My gaze could not reach that far.

We continued along in the darkness for some time more and then, suddenly, I felt my brother walk into my back as we stopped quickly in our tracks.

"There is a gap – the fence, look. It has been cut, look, look, Daina," said Father. His words sounded urgent and excited; they carried hope.

We all crouched around Father as he sought out a match; in its glare we could see where the cutters had twisted back the wire of the fence.

In the matchlight I saw my Father smiling broadly. He seemed bathed in glowing light, but then I watched his face change quickly to a hoary death-mask. My nerves jumped as Father called out with terror, "Jurgis!"

Father ran to my brother. I saw that Jurgis had fallen over; he was so small that I had not heard. Father scrambled with his matches and when I saw my brother's face his eyes no longer sparkled; they rolled up in his head.

Jurgis's lips turned blue with the cold. Where he lay on his back in the dampness his face looked so white that it could have been painted. I looked at my brother and he seemed as lifeless as a doll; I started to cry.

Father stood helpless above Jurgis and then Mother ran, throwing herself to her knees by his side. "Jurgis, Jurgis," she said over and over.

As mother held my brother's head close to her heart, her hand stroked violently up and down his back and slapped at his spindly little legs. "Jurgis, Jurgis, wake up," she said, "wake up, wake up, wake up."

I feared my brother must die. His face looked so rigid, as if set in bronze; seeing him like this felt like a sharp blade plunged in my heart.

My tears stopped for all of a minute as I thought of my brother, gone from us. I wondered if he was already in heaven, flying with the angels. It all seemed so wrong, I could not believe it.

I grew dizzy where I stood, swaying from toe to heel, but I would not have my brother taken from me. I had been his protector for too long to let that happen now. I must not be without him, I must not let him leave me, I thought.

I ran to my mother and screamed loud enough to waken death. I slapped and I slapped at my brother; his head lolled from side to side, my hands quickly became sore.

My mother did nothing. In the darkness her eyes shone like ripe berries, her teeth stuck tight against her lips, and then she disappeared. The matchlight expired and we fell into silence. If any one of us had taken a breath or a bird flapped a wing we would have heard it. And then came the dearest sound of my entire life.

My brother coughed. I felt him shift in my mother's arms. Father struck another match and when the light flooded in, Jurgis's face came alive again. My mother clung to him. She wept with joy as she stroked at his head over and over again.

Father took off this army greatcoat and wrapped Jurgis tightly within it. "Keep warm, my boy," he said, pressing out his chest and making a cradle of his hands, "keep warm and we shall be safe soon, I promise you, my son, we shall be safe soon."

As I listened to Father's words my eyes darted towards Jurgis, and then towards my mother. She frowned as Father spoke; she thought he had spoken too glibly.

"You cannot promise us that," said Mother, "you cannot promise."

The land seemed clothed in a purple light as we made our way across the ditch and found the old exporter, but my brother began to burn with fever once more.

Mother's hand trembled as she touched Jurgis's brow, wiping away the moisture with her coat sleeve. She bawled out at Father and cursed him for bringing us here. Her brows came together above her red-rimmed eyes. "Jurgis is just a boy," she said, her words rising like thunder, "he does not have the strength for this!"

Father stooped his head. He would not fight with her, but soon turned away to face the old exporter who led us from his counting room to a little wooden hut.

Inside the old exporter sat us by a black stove as he filled its pot-belly with coals. Mother held tightly to Jurgis, but she did not once look at the old exporter as he welcomed us, bringing rye bread and dark tea made with cut leaves and herbs.

It soon grew warm inside the hut and Mother wrapped camphor bandages around Jurgis's chest, all the while patting his head dry with her coat sleeve.

As my brother lay huddled by the fire in our mother's arms, I went over to look at him. He seemed very weak and pale. I took up his small hand and squeezed it tight.

Jurgis smiled at me and I smiled back, wishing him to be well soon. "Be strong, Jurgis," I said, "we will be in America soon, where we will see the shining motor cars."

My brother managed another weak smile, and I felt my heart seared in two.

In time the old exporter led us from his little hut to the grain store, where great mountains of amber-coloured grain stood piled high to the roof beams. Men shovelled the grain into burlap sacks, filling wicker crates like huge market baskets for loading onto the train. Everywhere the busy hum of activity drilled in my ears.

The old exporter moved quickly; his heavily creased black trousers became a blur beneath him. When he finally came to a halt he ran his fingers through his fine white hair and spoke. "And this, it is the hard part," he said through his crowded teeth, "the boy must travel alone."

Mother shook her head firmly; determination shone from her every pore. "The boy is too weak," she said, clutching Jurgis to her, "he will die with the cold. Do you hear me? He will die!"

The old exporter's hands moved nervously once more and then he hid them behind his braces, up on the bulge of his belly. "It has to be, we know of no other way," he said, "he must be sewn into the grain sack like all the rest; we know of no other way – there *is* no other way."

My mother held back her emotions, but I saw muscles twitching at the sides of her mouth. "He can be sewn in with me," she said loudly, "I will keep him warm with me."

"No, he cannot, the sack will not shut. Please, please," said the old exporter, "there are others too; would you have their lives be jeopardised in this way?"

My mother had no fight left in her; tears washed quickly over her high cheekbones. "Petras, please," she said. Mother's words scalded my heart but my father said nothing to her; his dark eyes alone said he could not have prised my brother from her clutches with irons.

As Father walked away, my mother's tears streaked down her face and her delicate shoulders trembled uncontrollably.

"Petras," my mother said, her voice as soft as a breeze, "Petras. Petras." She carried on with his name until her words faded into a whisper, and then she sobbed.

I went to my mother and brother and together we waited, in fear and silence, for Father to return. When he finally appeared he held up one of the burlap sacks we had seen. He seemed born of a new enthusiasm. "Myko get inside," he told me.

I did as Father asked, and then he pulled up the sack, over my head.

"See, you see, there is room enough for two of him in there," said Father, "you see, you see, my boys can travel together. Myko can keep Jurgis warm."

So, it was agreed this was how we must leave our homeland – sewn within grain sacks.

The goods train would carry us over the border and then we would be loaded onto the ocean liner like cargo. We would see no daylight for several days and when we felt the swaying of the seas beneath us, it meant we would soon be safe on America's shores, to begin our lives over.

Chapter Thirty-Four

My father loosed the remainder of his pack of hounds. They ran calling for my tiger's blood and latched quickly on his hinds and neck. I beat them off with my heavy gum branch. As a waddy it appeared a sound one; I saw my tiger flinch from its reach but the dogs kept coming back senselessly.

The smallest of the pack latched teeth on my tiger's throat. I felt sure this attack must soon bring the fight to an end, but then my father cruelly sought to extend his sport.

From within a tied-fast sack Father released my tiger's mate. She rushed to join the fray, snarling and lunging, her white fangs turning quickly blood-red. Together the tigers and I fought fiercely against my father's dogs.

"Get back! Back!" I shouted. My hands clutched tight to the waddy as I swung it through the air, again and again.

The earth felt scorched around us, the air close and musty, carried the fresh smell of blood. The blackened sky became deep hued as the night's doom closed on us. Threatening clouds gathered pace in the breeze; they did not burst, only pressed their weight upon us from on high.

"Back! Back!" I continued to shout to the dogs, but they did not tire; they knew who to take commands from.

All the while my father trained his eyes on the fight before him. The veins in his neck pulsed hard, followed by a throbbing in his temples which seemed to draw all emotion from his haunted eyes.

I watched his rifle keenly as I swung out with the waddy; he held it tight in his grasp, the tendons of his fist lit all the way to the knuckles by the fire's glow. I knew he tired of this sport – he had means to call its halt – but I must fight on for my tiger.

I swung out with the waddy time and again, I became a

machine, fighting for my tiger's survival. Nothing else mattered to me but the fight. And then, I heard the sudden sound of a rifle's crack sear the air.

"No," I called. I watched my tiger's mate fall.

My father had fired upon her spine, his shot was true to a hair. I knew this was a most painful way to die.

"No. No," I called again as I watched the tiger writhe and whine upon the ground, in her slow, cruel death throes. She raised a dust-cloud with her beating twists and turns; I could not watch her die this way.

"Finish her," I roared out to my father.

My tiger's mate fell face-down in the dirt, her defeat and agony plain to see. "Finish her," I called again, but my father stood mute. I knew he sketched plans to coax my respect as he stood raw-boned and calmly stroked the bridge of his nose. He raised up the rifle again, but this time he trained it on my tiger.

The fight had turned to my tiger and the last of Father's dogs and their fierce battle showed much strength was still held within them both. But the quick shifting of their limbs and claws dragged them before my father's aim. Until the last blow had been dealt, Father could not raise his rifle to take a shot. But, when it came, and my tiger tore the life from the defeated dog, I watched Father steady the rifle at his shoulder.

"No," I cried out.

My tiger's mate ceased her struggle on the ground below. She looked dark and shrunken, her last breaths strangled by the blood and dirt in her throat.

Father narrowed his cold eye upon the sight.

"No! No!" I called out to him again. I would not let him kill my tiger; he had won his fight, he had won his right to life.

Angry vibrations met my heart and my thoughts became crowded with my father's injustice. The atmosphere fell heavy with my hurt; not a sound came as I ran for my father with the waddy raised.

"You will not take my tiger!" I yelled.

I sensed my tiger caught in Father's gaze. He knew he faced the bearer of his death, and the one who stole his mate.

"Leave him be," I yelled, in the few leapt steps I took towards my father.

As I ran with the waddy raised it felt as if I ran from myself. The being I was stood calmly and watched another bring that gum branch down hard, upon my father's head.

"Myko," he said softly, as he slouched to his knees, and then fell before me.

As my father landed in the dirt, his gun cracked out and caught my tiger square on the chest. The bullet shattered bone; I heard its clacking as I watched him limp slowly back towards the forest depths.

"No!" I roared.

A shadow of misery fell upon my tiger as he crept timidly away, and then all was dark.

New fears quickly awakened in me and I felt my heart's heavy throbbing turn to stone beneath my chest. The rhythm of my breathing slowed, became shallow and silent, and then a trickle of tears began. I turned to my father, where he lay on the forest floor. In a glance, in just one brief moment where I held my father in my stare I believed the man he once was to be lost to me forever.

My father had taken too much from me now. I could not forgive him, my blood pumped a hate within me that I had never felt. As I stood squarely before him I heard my tiger struggling beyond in the gorse and I was overcome. I raised up the waddy and ran again for my father.

"You killed him! You killed him!" I yelled as I ran.

Father lifted himself onto his shanks to meet me; before

me his head bowed. I moved to bring the waddy down on his skull and crush out his life as easy as the lives he had taken himself.

"Why? Why did you kill him?" I cried uncontrollably as I forced out my words.

My thoughts and hurt rose like a continuous hammering. Tears rolled from my eyes and were whipped away by the wind as I ran. In my life, I had never before confronted my father with such harsh words.

"You are a murderer. You killed him. You killed my tiger just as surely as you killed my brother …"

I had let out all I stored in me.

The words entered my father's flesh as easily as stick-pins and the pain of them rose in his face. His eyes opened wide and white beneath the moon, but his pallor suddenly shrank dark and scaly.

He broke sweat quickly and his skin looked smeared with a heavy yellow oil. "No, Myko," said Father in a voice that did not seem to be his own, "no," he said again. The words sounded coarse in his throat. "No, it is not true."

"Yes. You killed him," I shouted, "you killed him. You killed him!"

I felt my hands tighten around the waddy; the smooth red gum wood felt as solid as steel in my palms. I lifted up my weapon and swung it in the air.

"You brought us here, you took us away. You forced us through the snow and the mud and the cold and brought Jurgis to his fever. It was you. You tied him within the sack … where *I* held him. I listened to his heartbeats weaken, listened to his breath growing heavier and heavier with every gasp he took. My brother died in my arms. My brother, my own brother … I felt his body turn to ice within my arms."

Father's mouth opened. He reached deep for words but

none came. His face turned to a tense mask of sorrow. His eyes, sunken deep and lifeless within their sockets, filled slowly with tears and then overflowed.

"You killed him. You killed him," I said.

Father bowed his head between his arms and wailed before me like a child. He dropped his face into the damp earth and shook violently. He writhed before me on the ground within his misery and as I stared I felt the waddy slip from my hands.

"You killed him," I said. "Jurgis was my brother and *you* killed him."

I had never seen my father this way. His bleak gaze sunken far inside his face cried of deep remorse and sadness.

"Just like you killed the tigers, just like you kill everything."

As I moved towards him and picked up his gun, I heard the landward waves giving in to the shore, beyond the crackling branches of the fire.

"Here, take this," I said.

I threw his gun to the ground, before him where he lay. "Take this, why don't you kill me, too? Just like you kill everything."

Father raised the gun I laid before him and cradled it in his arms. Stroking the gun gently he rocked back and forth, back and forth, sobbing all the while. I believed he had broken.

The sky above became black once again, the stars low and close as the clouds glided silently beneath them. The unspoiled forest beyond the clearing looked like a sinister place to me now. I felt my purpose once, but now I knew my efforts had failed. I was locked in my injuries and the hurt I felt was savage.

I turned from my father and as I moved I caught sight of a pale complexion, an ivory skin washed-up in the fire's light.

My mother pinned me with her eyes; whatever thoughts she held she kept to herself. Her hair was mussed by the wind, her eyelids heavy, but she stood as straight as a mullion-bar before me.

Slowly, she moved beyond the wattles; gnats dived on the lantern she held in her hand. I knew her fears must have driven her from the hut to follow the fire in the forest. But as I wondered how much of the night's conflict she had witnessed, I saw her grow stronger than I would have believed.

"You must stop," she said. Her words passed right through me, I could see they were for my father and I turned my head back towards where he lay on the ground.

Mother's voice rose higher; "You must stop," she said again; her words carried a strength I had never heard from my mother. They crashed like rocks falling from the steep cliff face. As she walked past me, Mother stood tall before my father and then, gently, she placed a hand on his face.

"I have failed, I have failed my family," said Father, "I should have paid my dues ... I should have gone back to the Czar."

My mother tightly held my father's head in her arms. "No! I told you to stay with me," she said; her voice echoed in the opening.

Father's head lolled on his heavy neck; his sobs grew louder and his back stood tense beneath his shirt. Father's great shoulders shook as he stuttered for speech. "How many have seen red snow?" he muttered beneath his tears. "How many? I have. I have seen it. Snow turned to blood, miles and miles all around, everywhere. I have seen a world washed with blood. A world washed with red from the veins of my countrymen."

"You must stop," said Mother once more, "raise yourself, raise yourself – you will not break."

My mother lifted my father onto his feet. "Do you hear me? You must stop, we need peace now."

"But ..."

"No, Petras. We need peace now."

Father looked on my mother where she stood before him, admonishing. She seemed to hold all the strength he had lost.

Father fixed her with his eyes. "I give you my oath. I give you my oath," he said. He cocked his head beyond where my mother stood between us and reached out a hand to me. "Myko," he said, "… my oath."

As I watched him a streak of rage pounded in me; I felt it a hurt to my heart to even look at him.

"You killed him," I said, "*you* killed him …"

As I spoke my mother turned around and softly called my name, but I was already gone from them both.

I ran for my tiger.

Chapter Thirty-Five

My tiger moved most slowly. I spied the blood he left on the man ferns and it did not take me long to latch on his trail.

I looked as far into the darkness of the forest as I could. Little light fell, save a thin white veil which lowered itself as softly as vapour from the pallid moon. My eyes settled over the trees; I saw the covering of hanging branches which reached out to the night's fringes like purple fingers.

As I moved through the high grasses and the deep rutted grooves of the dark scrub I felt the anger I held towards my father draining from me. The fire that roared within me was gone now, it had reached full flight and burned itself out.

The ground beneath my feet felt wet and the air smelled thick with my tiger's scent as I followed his steps. Disturbances filled the bush; I heard loud rustling noises that I knew to be beyond the usual reach of the night animals.

The ferocious wails of the dogs and the gunshots upset even the shore birds on the coast who took to the sky in panic, flying far beyond the breakers which lashed down upon the hard-packed sands and rocky shore slopes.

I stretched out my steps and took more of the island in every stride.

"I will find you, my tiger," I muttered, "I will find you."

Deep fatigue fell over me but I stood my pace through persistence. Since my tiger's wild flight the ebb of my emotions flowed to him and I sensed he wasn't far.

My tiger was wounded badly and each of his slow movements only prolonged the death that surely awaited him. I felt a flame rise again in my blood to think of my tiger's fate; I knew we had both now reached the fringes of our terror.

The land slipped low and rose again as I dropped the reach of my steps to make sure of my every footing. I saw possum scampering beneath me, over clods and through the dense covering of the bush, but I saw nothing of my tiger.

As I trudged wearily in my search I felt tears begin to roll down my face; they travelled slowly as my hurt reached its pitch.

"Where are you? Where are you?"

I knew I had lost much, my heart beat in chaos, my mind was a bale-fire I could not control.

"He has killed him!" I yelled out.

I thought to turn back, to confront my father once more, but I knew I would find no answers there. I felt a hard shell growing around the feelings I stored for my father. I now wished only to track my tiger as he made his final steps on his home range.

The ground of the woodland become wetter and the soil, a mire. As I stumbled awkwardly I felt a cold blade of loss press on my throat and then, suddenly, I was taken by surprise; I fell upon my tiger.

A short wheeze emitted from far below his chest, his every painful step put needles in my eyes. I could not watch his suffering. I wanted to raise my tiger and rest with him where we stood but I knew his pacings were something he would not give up.

His trail through the bush was a well-travelled one, though I believe we both knew he would not come this way again.

As I watched my tiger's painful steps I felt my conscience swell inside of me as smoothly as a tide's change; I knew I was part of the cause. I had lived under the roof of my father, who claimed near fifty tiger bounties and hunted and harmed I did not know how many more. I took shelter from the Van Diemen's Company which paid out on tiger scalps and worst of all, throughout, I had done nothing. Even when my tiger, perhaps the last grown male of his kind, came looking for my protection, I failed him truly.

"I am sorry," I told my tiger. "I am sorry, I am sorry." My tears streamed on my face as I looked down at him, his slow gait turning to a pathetic stumble. I knew the steel within him had begun to fail. He had only one purpose now: his own grim survival through the prevailing moments.

"I swore to protect you, and I have not," I said softly, "you were so brave … you took the greatest risk to call on me. You showed your strength – you were so brave."

Even now as I gazed upon my tiger's blood-wet back, his slow ungainly limp through the blackwood wattle seemed one of greatness. I knew we neared his lair and I saw my tiger as a warrior who had fought and lost, and returned home, to die.

The urgent dawn awoke and blue air floated all around us. The myrtles stood tall in the wet gullies and the pebble-smooth hills rose above the highest of the treetops and caught the early sun's shine. The path ahead divided into sunlight and shadow beneath a vault of heavy branches as the stirring heat shimmered low to the ground.

A soapy white froth gathered around my tiger's jaws as he swung his legs heavily towards his final resting place. He gave a low snort from his blunt nose and a bloodied drool emitted before him.

He fell slowly in his movements now; his dulled eyes seemed to view me from a great distance as we came upon his hide. The lair was silent; no movement save the cold breeze before us touched its rings of crowded branches.

My tiger did not have the strength to lift himself over its edge. I looked away. I could not watch this once mighty creature lowered to such a state of pity.

His hinds failed him as he tried to leap within, and soon he was forced to drag his wounded body forward, as he writhed like a lizard, over the lair's edge. All the while my tiger's eyes looked front. He held a purpose in his mind which stoked his courage and gave him strength, but I knew it would soon be spent.

As I watched my tiger fall below the lair's edge, he lay on its floor for several long minutes. I believed he was dead. He merely wished once again to seek the familiar aspect of his lair, to die in his own place.

"I have lost you," I said.

I could not make my limbs carry me to where my tiger lay. I knew he lay as dead as the ages. I did not need to see his eyes, now dimmed and lifeless.

My body trembled as if suddenly I had leapt from a fireside into the outdoors of a winter's cold. I struggled in dark eddies of grief, my only thought of how my tiger had suffered.

I raised up my hands, tried to jolt my senses by slapping my face with my open palms, but it was useless. I could not shake myself from this moment. It was no imagining, it was as real as the salt tears which ran down my face.

"No," I cried out. "No, it can't be true. Why? Why?"

In the moment of my tiger's death I longed to join him. Wherever he may be, in heaven or only as clay, I wished to be as dead.

My face became contorted. I felt the curl of my mouth and my brow. I do not know what shape my face took but I had seen terror and grief before and I guessed I held the worst of both.

My tremblings became uncontrollable and I dropped fast to my knees and faced hellwards. I convulsed where I lay on the ground in heavy tears. My tiger was gone.

"No. No. No," I cried to myself.

I hit at the ground, the wet and dark of the soil came into my eyes and my mouth. I wished for it to cover me, bury me where I lay. I did not deserve this life, I would die, please God I would die.

At some point in my despair, in the pit of my wild hurt I sensed a movement in the bush.

I did not raise my head. Were I to be mauled by devils, they could have my flesh without resistance. Let them feast on me as they would surely now feast on my tiger.

My neck was touched. It felt like a smooth hand, the soft hand of my mother perhaps, gently cajoling me to resume this existence, but I could not rise. My neck was touched a second time. This time the feel was harsher, like a claw. As I lifted myself I saw little. My eyes seethed with mud, but as I rubbed at their edges I saw the most beautiful sight I had ever seen.

"You are alive," I whispered.

If I lived to be a hundred I do not believe I could ever feel such joy again. As my eyes adjusted to the sight before me I was lifted on the wings of angels.

My tiger had raised himself from within his lair. In his mouth he held his cub, which he presented to me, as if it were my rightful son. I took the cub in my arms. I held it beneath my tears and stroked the warm softness of its downy coat. And then I watched my tiger rest, as he would forever more.

Chapter Thirty-Six

The same cruel breeze which carried my tiger from me blew all around. I felt its sharp edges like thorn branches and I knew at once I must leave this place.

The heat and glare rose, and flies began to settle on my tiger's bemused stare. I swallowed my hurts, but I was stiff and desolate as I raised up my tiger's body and placed it in the lair. As I laid my tiger down I saw the small body of another cub inside. It was a female, smaller than the male beneath my coat; it still felt warm, its weak body had not long succumbed.

I placed the small tiger within my shirtfolds to comfort the live cub, which nuzzled to be nearer the familiar scent. I did not disturb the lair any more. My tiger had chosen it well; I did not believe it would be found by any man. His hide would not be torn unless devils devoured it, which they most surely would.

I stood before my tiger's lair and watched the light, with smooth precision, cut jagged curves into the hidden resting place. All around the sun polished the silver gum trunks and the peculiar air fell gritty with dust. I heard the river running low and deep in its time-eaten banks, and as the lofty breeze sang overhead I felt a deep heart-hurt ball up inside me.

The heat-swayed trees shimmered under the monotone blue sky as I took a last glance upon my tiger's remains. The sun's rays fell in intricate honeycombs at my tiger's lair, but it was not him anymore.

"Goodbye, my tiger," I whispered.

As I ran on fresh limbs my mind functioned with a clarity I had not known for some time. The coldness of my heart felt like a mechanical functioning; what was left inside me contained no feeling. I grew consumed by purpose – my tiger would have his final glimpse of freedom, through the eyes of his young cub.

The blue of the sky leeched the colour from the clouds and the sunlight travelled slowly in the forest as I crashed through the branches. I wandered into the teeth of a headwind which carried a misty spray in the wide glades and widening track-runs and I soon found myself on the turnpike road to home.

I stripped possum from my father's snares and tried to feed the cub.

"Eat up," I said quietly, "try it, try it."

The cub, more accustomed to feeding from his mother, took only nips of flesh at first, but soon he surprised me and ate feverishly. I felt proud to have provided for him in this way, but I knew his trials were just beginning.

As I swung my legs over the sagging fence wires of my family's holding the crude split-paling hut hove into view. I hoped my mother and father had not returned home yet, but if they were there I was ready to confront them once more. Nothing would stand in my path; I knew I must bank my pride and draw some supplies.

As I trod the red-earth path to home my mouth grew dry. The air became stilted as I approached. The sun pressed a bar of sharp light on the hut's door and I felt my breathing heavy as I walked towards the dwelling. A deepening blackness drew around me with every inch I took, but as I stepped inside, the hut was empty.

I tried to fill a burlap sack with the few goods my mind seized upon: a lantern, a jute rope, flour, a water canister. All the while the cub slept soundly beneath my shirtfolds. I felt the warmth of his contented breath; the cub understood nothing of my fears.

"Rest up now," I whispered as I patted at his back, "rest up there."

I hoped the cub's full belly would allow him to sleep for a long time as I clutched on the sack and hurried from my home.

Outside in the holding yard the station's grey mare stood calmly picking at stray tufts of grass on the ground. She seemed peaceful as I saddled up and climbed on her back. I dug my heels in hard and soon the dark-red of the earth turned to dust as I made my tracks from this place.

I knew I would not return for a long time, if ever. My thoughts grew focused, my mind waged on a new cause, but as I rode out to put my plans in place I knew there to be little else I could control.

I felt far removed from the goings of the world. I remembered how I once read of the Indian rope trick, and saw pictures of men suspended on the air. I imagined that this was how I functioned: as though I floated high above the ground, high above my normal thoughts in a state few ever reach.

My coat-tails flew in the air as the grey thundered on beneath the opal sky.

"Get up! Yah!" I yelled, as we trampled heavily through the fields of bracken and the dirt tracks to the townships. The heat picked up fiercely and long red flames grew from the outcrop of the sun's gloryburst.

Open collared, I felt my skin tingle from too long spent in the sun, but I would not slow or stop – I knew phantoms pursued me across the unbroken emptiness of the landscape.

The farther from home I travelled, the more I understood. Soon, I felt a new idea running in my mind like verse. When I thought of it, it had always been there. It felt as if I had always been figuring it out, trying its merits and also its faults, but it did not seem like any normal idea of mine. This was the type of thing my brother had once planned in our games. As boys we ran into the forest and became soldiers, using sticks for our guns; I often played at such games with my brother.

"When I grow up," I remembered Jurgis had said, "I will take part in battles."

"And so will I. We will both fight in great armies and get medals for our chests."

We would be soldiers of such honour, not like our conquerors. We planned our manoeuvres like great commanders, with raids, daring raids on unseen enemies, but always we were the victors, always our plans were superior.

Jurgis, how I wish you were with me now, I thought. As close as either of us would now come to our dreams, as near to such honour as we would approach, was now in my hands.

I pressed the grey harder than I should have; by our journey's end her flanks were streaked with sweat and red with dust. But the grey had a strong back and a good heart and carried her exertions with little care.

I'd never travelled so far from home on my own and here was a strange new place to me; I knew little of the streets of the city of Hobart.

In the blue sky above, a white sickle of moon sat beside the dimming amber of the sun's glow. Motor vehicles filled up the roads. I had never encountered cars or trucks traveling the northern sheep runs and I became overcautious, making many jerkings on the grey.

I saw people watch me closely. I felt their eyes, and I saw their reading of the Van Diemen's Company ensign on the grey's hind. I had no right to this mount and their looks felt threatening, but I found courage to test their doubts.

I approached an officer of the law; his features looked shrunken, his boots and uniform covered in road dust. "I need directions to the Beaumaris Zoo," I said.

If the officer had suspicions of me, he showed none.

"On horseback?" he said; his voice crackled with rheum.

I replied quickly, "Yes, sir."

The officer plainly tipped his helmet. "Then it'll be a chore, there are a heap of streets to cross, but I can set you about the right course."

He made many gestures, pointing all the while to landmarks I must pass. "Just follow your nose from there," he said when done.

"Thank you, sir," I said. I felt grateful for his kindly help, and for the chance to test my calm before authority. I knew I must hold my emotions in check now.

My father said he had sold the female tiger and her cubs that he trapped to the zoo. I had no reason to doubt that he had kept his word to me to spare the tigers' lives, but I trusted nothing to be as it should be now.

I do not know why I harboured such doubts about my father. I knew him as a man of his word, but my mind filled with grim imaginings and I felt forced to examine every avenue of fate.

I had taken a track which had already brought much suffering, to more than just myself. I had stolen the grey and raised a hand to my own father. However, these crimes seemed petty considerations to me. I would face their consequences later; as I pressed on, my mind fixed on a higher law, one which occupied me in the strangest of ways.

Chapter Thirty-Seven

The sinking sun shone cheerlessly as it towed the remaining brightness from the day. The wind breezed up again and the flat yellow-stone buildings turned flinty grey when they met the reddened light. All around the magpies cawed and took the day's last chance to dig for grubs and grasshoppers. Dust powdered the streets and the smell of horses moving all around came upon the air at every turn.

My mouth felt dry and my lips clung to my teeth as I tethered the grey. I left my tiger's cub sleeping curled as quiet as a lamb within a robust hollow trunk.

"Rest up, now," I said. I gave the cub my coat to keep him warm and he had his sister's scent and soul to guard him in my absence.

I did not want to leave him, but I knew that I had to. I knew I must keep a cold gaze in each eye I placed on the cub. He was no dog pup, but a beast of the wild and my aim was to maintain him that way. Clinging like a mother hen towards her broody roost would not help raise this cub, which faced struggles in the wild when left alone, with perhaps none of his own to turn to.

Brisk clouds lunged overhead as I walked light-footed through the thinning angles of sunlight. Some warmth held in the day's remaining hours and the air turned syrupy. Hobart's wide streets looked pleasant and the people I crossed seemed keen to salute me, but I kept my expression motionless. I felt trapped in an anxious dream and kept a slim plank's breadth of track all the way to the Beaumaris Zoo.

I did not take me long to discover my father had kept his promise to me, but the sight that greeted me came as a heart-scald. If other animals, save tigers, were caged within the confines of the zoo, I did not record their type. I came only to find the tiger my father had sold.

Few others paid interest to the tiger or her cubs, save an old cove who hovered at my shoulder. The beasts had little life within them, lain upon the straw in their cage like sacks of grain. Their faces revealed the life within them slowly drained away; their eyes looked as dead as those of mounted stag heads.

"No beast enjoys the confines of such a place," said the old cove at my side, "but tigers, I believe, fare worse than most."

I turned to face him, he was tall and broad, his white whiskers teased up towards his pink cheeks.

"Look at these laughing hyenas," said the old cove as he swiped a hand at the crowds with their fingers pointed at the shamed animals, "I want to be no part of this gawping throng of ghouls!"

"Then why are you here?" I snapped.

The old cove turned to me and smiled, his pink cheeks blushed red, "You have me there boy," he said, "you have me there."

I saw the young female tiger leave the cover of her cubs to pace the cage for a few brief moments. She looked in a daze as she crept towards the four walls, each after the other, as if in disbelief of the limits of her surroundings.

"There's no sadder sight than a predator, suited to roam far across plains and rugged lands, caged and forced to feed from the end of a broom handle," said the old cove.

As he spoke I watched the tiger pacing, and I saw that now she had only two cubs. I wondered how long it would be before the other cubs perished. Then what would be left of the tigers?

"They will not last here," I said.

"Few tigers survive in such conditions, my boy. None have ever been bred in this way."

The old cove removed his stockman's hat and brushed at its brim; little specks of dust gathered in the air before him.

"But there's few tigers now will ever find their way towards this life of misery," he said.

"They are too few," I snapped.

"Too few, my boy, they are as good as gone."

I turned to face the old cove but he was fixed on the tigers before us, his pale watery-blue eyes wandering back and forth with each step the tiger took.

"This zoo once kept a steady trade in tigers, shipping them around half the globe and paying the trappers well for their haul. But now, my boy, those days are coming to a close. You could be setting eyes on one of the last."

The old cove's voice fell thin and reedy as he spoke. For a moment I wondered if he would shed a tear, and then he turned and tipped his hat to me.

"Good day to you, young sir," he said, and then he was gone.

I sat for nearly an hour watching the caged and saddened tigers by myself. I sensed little connection between us. I hoped for the same response I once shared with my now dead tiger, but hardly an acknowledgment passed from the dark eyes of the female and her remaining cubs.

In time a small finch wandered between the bars of the tiger's cage and suddenly the female became suffused with life, latching on the tiny bird with her long claws. For an instant she became alive again. As she shook the finch by the head a dim glow fired her eyes, and then she lowered the bird towards her cubs; a moment later, she resumed her look of torpor.

I could not watch anymore, and raised myself from the ground. I moved forward to place my hand through the bars of the cage, the tiger sensed no threat and did not raise her head to me. I watched her eyes alight on me for a moment but I had become just another fixture within the limits of her meagre world.

"I'm sorry you must suffer this way," I said calmly.

I left the tiger to her gloom, and returned to my own tiger's cub. I found him curled soundly in the coat I had left him in, but he had moved far from his sister's cold, still body. I believe he accepted her absence from him.

I tried to feed some possum to the cub, but he ate nothing this time. I had no desire for food myself – my stomach was now turning over like a steamer paddle with the task I faced.

Stars appeared in the sky. They looked like little piercings on a curtain which shielded us from the daylight. As I gazed up I wondered was this world becoming weary? Was the night sky really as threadbare as an old woman's shawl?

I knew there had been much lost on this earth already, but since the passing of my tiger I felt each loss and its pain anew.

How can such a thing be mended? I did not know the answer. Surely once a thing is gone, taken from the world, it cannot return.

I imagined the things my tiger must have seen, the seasons he lived through, the joys he surely felt. I knew my tiger's story as if it were my own. I still remembered well what the friendly bosun first told me, as we made our way to my tiger's island.

"Tigers once numbered here in their thousands, it was their refuge, sought from the main," he had said.

"There were tigers on the mainland, too?" I had asked.

"Yes, oh yes. They were content to roam there once, but man drove them far from that home."

The bosun's story fascinated me.

"How?" I asked. "How did they drive out the tigers?"

"When the earliest settlers arrived, many thousands of years ago, they brought dogs – and the dogs were hunters."

"The dogs fought with the tigers?"

"The dogs hunted in the tigerlands; they didn't care how they came by a kill, they were carrion eaters too, not like the tigers – the tigers had their pride, they ate only what they killed."

"So the tigers were starving?" I asked.

"When the dogs thrived, the tigers fled over the last slender needle of land before the rising seas separated the main, creating the island." The bosun had pointed to the island. I still saw his face cut by the sun as he spoke.

"On this island the tigers survived for thousands of years more, in peace, before man arrived in his tall ships and set the cycle once more in its throes."

I felt every hurt of the tigers' sad plight because we all had a share in this slaughter. Every man on the island had brought down the tigers, every soul had turned against them where they roamed.

I saw youngsters playing, some barely walking, and knew at once they were taught to fear and kill the tigers. I had listened to the stories in the billet at Woolnorth, from the peddlers on the wayroads and in the chatterings of shop girls. None felt emotion for the tigers' cause. The tiger was raged against, and for what?

I remembered the old cove's words and I longed to pick up my tiger's cub and hold it like a babe, to cry into its downy fur like a child, but I could not. This tiger cub was all the tigers' last chance, and I clearly understood that; I could not risk aligning it with any man, even myself. I must see that the tiger cub survived on its own, far from any fear or threat from mankind.

All along the road's curve the milky moon laid down a waxy layer of skin that grew into the dark distance and then disappeared. Black-coloured buildings were cut out against the dark-grey of the horizon and stretched upwards to the sky's line. I felt a chill of fear as I embarked upon the most recent of my crimes, but I steadied my nerves. I knew I must resist the call of my conscience and get on with what I had to do; I would gladly commit more grievous wrongs than this to reach my aim.

As I proceeded my steps fell slow but persistent. The wind veered into my path and put a damp coldness in my bones, but I raised my pace and my heated blood soon brought a warm glow to my face. It did not take long before I put an eye on my target.

I watched and waited for the last of the lights to dim and finally be drawn to darkness at the Beaumaris household and then I marched into the yard.

I pushed at the iron filigrees of the gateposts – they held no locks or fastenings – the hinges, recently greased, made little sound as I entered. I came prepared to climb fences and walls, to cut through chains, but I found myself admitted to the zoo's keep as freely as a paying customer.

I knew my aim, I rehearsed it well. I sought out the female tiger and her cubs without faltering in my steps. I anticipated much commotion from the creatures but they greeted me as no threat. I felt blessed to walk among these animals and rouse no emotion save the occasional curious glance in my direction.

New sleek waves of calm washed over me as the tiger seemed to greet me when I showed; I sensed understanding in her eyes. I knew she was not glad to see me, but perhaps she felt resigned to play her part in my new fate.

I reached beyond the bars once more and she let me rest my hand on her head, "Hello there," I whispered, "hello my girl."

For some long moments we stared at each other in the stillest of understanding, and then she removed herself to the back of the cage.

As the tiger went, I silently climbed to the rear of the

enclosure and unlatched the cage's bolt-fastening. The tiger did not stir, but her two cubs ran from out the darkness to whimper at her rear. I felt shamed to bring them fear, but the tiger soon calmed her cubs, licking on their ears.

The air came thick with a musky tiger scent as I went inside the cage. It felt cramped, as I crawled on all fours my back scratched on the roof. My heart beat loudly in my chest and fresh fears blistered on my mind. As my shoulder blades crowded closer together, my thoughts suddenly formed into a new shape. I felt for the poor tiger within these walls, but I believe she knew what I planned.

"Good girl," I whispered again, "good girl."

From beneath my shirtfolds I removed the dead cub and placed it on the ground before her. At once the tiger clawed the cold cub closer and tried to make out its scent. Her blunt-nose twitched noiselessly, and then her heavy eyelids raised several times in curiosity. When she had completed her inspection, the tiger once more placed licks on her cubs. The cubs seemed curious to see another of their kind within the cage and drew closer to its side.

The cubs looked matched for size with the dead tiger, both being female, and still very small. I knew I could withdraw one freely – the dead cub making a sound match for its missing number.

It seared my heart to remove the tiger cub from its mother and sister, its plaintive cries reached deep within me as I buried the cub beneath my shirtfolds. The cub's mother did not watch as I left her behind, but I felt the eyes of the young sibling as it squatted deep within the straw, as if unbelieving of another loss.

"Goodbye," I said, "I will take good care of her."

Though I felt their pain I knew I must not take them all. My task must go unnoticed by man, nothing could be risked that might betray my plans. As I ran down the stony dust-packed path I felt sure I had done right. I now held two tigers to pair in the wild. If there was a chance for these tigers to grow and survive, then perhaps I could yet fulfil my own dead tiger's wishes.

Chapter Thirty-Eight

Clouds crossed the sky on the breeze and thin shadows shambled beneath the hill rises and plateau flats. In this sun-buoyed day the clammy air felt hot all around. The light streamed through the drooping branches and shining leaves, and the forest colours penetrated even the darkest shadows of the thick vegetation, where blocks of sunlight stacked high on the tree stems.

I headed for the central plateau, a land unseen by man, occupying most of the island's middle share. Its western parts form the mountain ranges which extend all the way to the southern coast. They are not high mountains, but very rugged, their gullies and river valleys holding a steep incline covered in thick rainforest.

I found no roads or tracks as I travelled. "This is rough country," I muttered to myself.

Any tracks carved by bushcutters grew over after only a few days. I knew this as a desolate place for men. As the bushlands opened out I still found no trampled ways. Even returning to the forests' light-breaks, where the grasses grew high, no signs of man's movements showed.

I took the higher country, where the open areas of sedgeland held the strands of forest surrounding the utmost ridges. The plains were not extensive, they occurred with frequency, but at their breadth spread only a few hundred yards apart.

I knew the rain fell heavily here; at all times of the year it landed in drops the full width of a man's hand. In such a place, all progression is difficult; hereabouts all farming is impossible.

I see now why no settler ever put down here. In such large areas of wooded seclusion, there are many places which offer security for tigers, and quiet, for breeding. The country here is rich in marsupials, there are large wallaby populations, wombats and brush possums also. These are lands where tigers can hunt, feed themselves well, and roam over a large area, unhindered by any fear of man.

I knew this to be the best place for the cubs as I headed for the deep and desolate lands, surrounded by the dark hollows of the mountain gums and the coverings of bracken patches on the forest floor.

My haul of tiger cubs curled together in the open saddle-bag I had latched tightly to the grey. Brief moments when they bristled with energy arose now and then, but mostly they lay sleepy-eyed and quiet. Though they seemed content I knew that they faced many trials. Any chance for the cubs to survive without their parents was slight. I had hopes they might grow well, that the land would support them, but the task lay heavily on my thoughts.

By the time the sky grew grey beneath the tarnished moon I felt drowsy with fatigue. I had travelled through the night and an entire day when I set down to rest by a shallow river. The water flowed fast and fish thrashed as I let the cubs stretch out their legs.

"Go, run about," I called to them, "get used to this place, it will be your home ... I hope, forever."

The noise from the tinkling stream occupied the cubs for a time as they raised up their small noses and sniffed furiously. But as I moved to gather dry twigs for a fire they started to trail me.

Underneath the hazy stars the cubs became tangled in the high sedge and I had to raise them, bleating, by their scruffs.

"Out of there," I called to the cubs. Their antics amused me, but did not take me from my fears for long.

I tried to feed the cubs bullock livers, which I carried

231

within my supplies, but both seemed unsure of my offering.

"What's wrong with it?" I said. I talked more and more to them; with each word their ears twitched and their heads lolled from side to side to better make out what I said.

"Here, try it …" I coaxed them towards the bullock livers but they merely looked at me with wide confused eyes.

"Okay, I will eat them." My father used this trick to cajole a sick dog to its tucker tray. As I knelt down the cubs became curious, sniffing at my ears to see what I had hidden from them.

"Ah, I have your attention now," I said, "I see …"

I raised up their feed in my teeth and they leapt to grab their share; then soon ate their fill like hungry wolves.

Together, at the start of our new adventure, I knew the cubs to be delicate creatures that carried many fears. I knew that I did too. I had no idea how my plans for them would unfold, but I knew we must all learn together if we were to have any chance of survival.

In the still of morning I awoke to find the cubs snugly stored beneath my shirtfolds. I did not know how they found their way there, but I moved quickly to discourage such behaviours and pushed them away from me.

"Get down. Away! Away!" I said. I was careful not to raise my voice too high and frighten them. "Go away! You have your own sleeping space in the hay I put down for you. Go away. Go away!"

I watched the cubs lumber off, brushing the grasses, until they stood with bemused stares by the brink of the glassy stream. As I watched them, beneath a knot of foliage on the river's bend, the cloven air fanned their curiosity. The cubs grew deeply interested in their new surroundings and the thought gored me. I knew I must act quickly to encourage their natural instincts.

A bold cloud eclipsed the sun and I saw we had camped

close by a high cliff, drawn in black. Through the chinking light I saw its bare surface seemed as smooth as marble; it looked like just the kind of isolated place I hoped to find.

I picked up the cubs and headed through the forest's unbroken hum towards the cliff. The sky above stretched blue, scrubbed clean of clouds, and the air grew sticky. Curved blades of light cut through the canopy and reed-sheaves whistled by the slapping water banks.

When we reached the cliff's steep face, the sun's glow leaned firmly on the highest of the crags. I made for a narrow cave set low in the ridge's wall. Inside a rectangle of yellow light cut a trapdoor on the cave floor. I kept the cubs to the rear and collected a nest of branches and leaves, like my tiger had made. They grew not to fear me now, raising their hinds and dropping their paws and heads each time I returned to the cave, but I discouraged their playfulness.

"Away, back, back," I said. This turned out to be my hardest task, to rebuff the cubs when they offered me affection, but I could not risk them bonding to me. Soon the cubs would need to fend for themselves. Though they filled me with pride and my heart puffed full every time I looked down at their tawny faces and playful chestnut eyes I knew our destinies were not bound together. We had to be parted soon enough, and I knew that would be a painful day.

Chapter Thirty-Nine

I snared possum and tried to feed the cubs as a grown tiger might. They took my gifts in a peculiar fashion. I laid a possum before the cubs and the one I presented the bait to took it and fed first, whilst the other merely watched. Neither cub fought the other for food. The pair seemed nothing like dogs, who when delivered their feed will attack one another to get the greatest share. My young tigers did not quarrel with each other.

I tried to train them to feed themselves with wounded possums from the snare lines, but they merely drew sport from the poor creatures.

"No, it is not a toy," I called out to them, as they shook the possum, and passed it between them like a rag doll.

I tired of their antics and wondered if I had made a dreadful mistake. Grim thoughts splintered in my mind: what if I cannot teach these animals to hunt like their true parents? Then how will they fend in the wild without me?

I did not want to be the tigers' defender all my life. I longed to see them run free, to take up the challenge of their own lives without me. Though it filled me with joy to watch the tigers growing strong, I held many fears and I wondered how much longer I could continue to keep them in this way.

I grew panic-ridden; in time they would surely starve – what might I be in the eyes of my tiger then? I could not face the thought that I would carry my tiger's hopes into hell.

Suddenly at my lowest ebb, as I felt soon to be engulfed by my fears, a remarkable thing happened. Like the peaceful gush of a stream I felt my heart suddenly lightened as I woke startled in the noisy night. I turned a lantern on the walls and floor of the cave to find it alive with writhings and squeals.

Dark shadows moved like a black sheet of water in ripples.

I saw tiny shining points of steel breaking everywhere the light fell. For a moment I felt confused, my mind became a stony lump of flesh that would not function, and then, I regained my senses.

My first instincts gave me over to fears, but I quickly remembered I was the cubs' protector and drew a latch on my emotions. As I did this it became dimly visible that a large pack of rats set about nesting in our cave.

Great numbers of the beasts swarmed everywhere my gaze fell. I toyed with the idea of an attack. I stood up and stamped my square-toed boots down on the nearest of the intruders but my efforts made little effect. I knew too many filled the cave for me to kill. I feared I must find a new place to rest and begin afresh with my efforts to raise the cubs.

"It's no good. It's no good," I yelled.

As a ghost-like ray came down from the moon and glided into the cave, the disquiet suddenly disappeared and I felt my heart glow warm.

As if a hunting instinct was suddenly born in the cubs, they flew upon the rats, catching them in their jaws, killing them soundly and with great speed. I saw their brown-timbered limbs had grown strong, their backs sinewy and deep-muscled beneath their thickening coats.

"Yes, that's it," I yelled out, "that's the way. Round them out. Round them out!"

The cubs' claws moved swiftly and their lunges chased the direction of their prey faster than the darting of an eye. As I watched I knew my mouth gaped like a hooked fish, and then a vague joy thrust into my mind and I felt a smile travel slowly over my face.

"That is the way. That is the way," I said softly.

I shook, wracked with tears of pride, as I watched the cubs clear the cave of the last of the rats.

When done, the cubs felt sufficiently exerted to feast upon their catch. As they collected their prizes I knew now they could survive without me – now that they had learned the taste of blood. Together, my tiger cubs would learn to hunt and kill for themselves.

"I will have to keep you hungry now," I told them, "if you are to continue to feed yourselves."

In the days that followed the cubs grew tired through the day, sleeping like lap dogs in the cave. I knew they had changed fast.

At night they wakened me as they climbed over where I lay, and made their way into the darkness to hunt.

Months passed and the cubs quickly grew stronger. Their coats lost their downy fur and became heavy, the male turned bronze-coloured and stood a foot taller than the lime-pale female.

As I rested alone in the desolate sweep of the forest, I knew the tigers were now strong enough to fend for themselves. They did not need me. It came as a deep hurt to know I must soon leave them. I tried to push away the thought of losing my tigers as the failing sun dropped weak rays that failed to put warmth into the musty air. I raised my eyes to the gnarled shapes of the isolated cliffs and watched the soft blue edges of the sky seep into nothingness. The stream washed over the supple gum branches that dipped above the banks and I wondered if I had let myself stay longer with the tigers than I should have. I needed to be sure the tigers had no need for me, but in my heart, I knew they were capable of fending for themselves.

"They do not need you now, Myko," I said aloud.

The shade detached itself from the wall of trees that I stood beside and enveloped me in new chills. The stream tinkled on and I strained my eyes on its glazed surface. I did not want to leave the tigers. They still approached me and nuzzled their snouts in my face but their absences had grown lengthened, and they no longer dwelled within the cave.

It is time to let them go, I thought.

The weak sun fell below the highest rock pile on the horizon and the rigid cliffs darkened in shadow. As I looked on I felt a growing desolation in my heart. I knew that the tigers had become a part of me and I still longed for contact with them. They were my family now, and I grew sick with loneliness.

I knew that I'd turned away from my own people. I confronted my father, and then fled from my family. Could I ever return to my home again? The notion ran in my mind over and over again.

Deeply felt guilt for my actions stabbed at my memory daily. I had turned on my own father and brought him down with blows. Had he only been trying to lead his family to safety, just like my tiger?

Whenever I closed my eyes I saw one thing only: my father sobbing before me, his drooping moustaches catching the wet tears of a broken man.

As the dying red sun bled over the landscape I lay my head down in a patch of moss. I heard the high-pitched screams of the currawongs as they returned to their bowl-shaped nests, high in the tree branches. Each cry from above jabbed a sharp point into me and I knew fears that I could not halt rattled in my bones.

Soon the darkening sky drank up all the light for miles around and black clouds burst above; their rain came clouting on my head as heavy as falling stones. My unkempt hair hung lank and wet before my eyes as I made my way back to the shelter of the cave. I loped like an ape through the forest as mud currents ran in shoals and channels at my feet.

The cave was dark as I entered and I quickly lit the lantern.

The dim glow of the light shone on the walls, drawing a fluttering of gnats, and at once I felt a new presence. The male tiger stood before me, he had brought a possum kill into the cave and he laid it at my feet.

I must leave. I knew this in an instant. The tiger had come to see me as his responsibility. This adult provider thought me a part of his fold. I did not want to break the bond between us, but I knew I must now sever it forever.

"Out! ... Go! Out of here!" I roared and yelled before the tiger like a mad man.

I raised a great mayhem before the male tiger. I bared my teeth and increased my roars.

"Out of here! Go! Scat! Scat!"

The tiger ran flinching from the cave to his mate. They both held me with great, sad eyes, uncomprehending of my wild appearance. I knew the time had come to convince them of the terror within man and I turned upon them fiercely.

"Scat! Scat!" I bellowed, my teeth bared, my whole being wild with fright.

The tigers fled quickly, their ears pressed low to their heads. They could not believe me to be the same creature that had fed and sheltered them as young.

I chased them through the mountain gums, clipping fast on their tails. I growled as well as any animal could, and caught the female by her hinds.

She rolled on to her flank, her pouch creased, and I saw her belly bulge with a new life. At once I sunk my teeth in her coat and drew a bite of hair. She yelped. I did not pierce the flesh, but I wished her to believe I would.

The male sensed her distress and took his own bite from the air before my face: a warning, but the pain was great to see him attack me in this way. I persisted: "Go away. Run. Scat!" I roared.

I watched the pair break for the forest, and at speed they ran from me. I roared again at their descent below the cover of man ferns. Neither made a backward glance; I believed I had turned them as well as I could from me. I wanted them to feel only fear of me; and to fear all I stood for.

"You must go. Go from me," I said, as my words turned quickly to sobs.

The sky above fell rain-washed and heavily clouded. The stuttered sound of the stream gathered itself into a roar as it crashed on the smooth polished rocks and rose high above its banks.

"You must get away from me," I sobbed, "you must get away."

I took myself back towards the cave as the heavens opened and I watched the billabongs turn from flat slabs of polished stone to fierce boiling stove pots. When I reached the cave, wet depressions gathered on the muddy floor and rippled their way further afield with every slap of the cruel wind.

In the days to come the sun made few appearances, it merely coasted dimly along with the flounces of cloud. Green shoots sprang up among the mess of wattles and beneath the tree stems, where blowflies lodged themselves in the black, wet bark gaps.

As I stared out on the plateau, I saw nothing of the tigers. I knew their joyful presence had left the cave forever. I turned them out and turned them far from me.

"Stay away from the likes of me, tigers," I said into the wind, "stay far away."

I knew I must leave now. I had no more to do. If there was work left, it was the tigers'. My hopes for them rose high, but my heart felt riven and cut to know I could never see them again.

The air turned sharp and cold, nipping in my throat and eyes as I stared out across the wild unselected country. I tried to imagine how the tigers would roam, and perhaps find the remaining few of their kind.

I cheered to think that they would thrive, that my own tiger received his wish. "You were a most cunning beast. Any tigers that come from you will surely be wise," I said. "Perhaps they will know to keep far from man."

For myself I had no such hopes; I lapsed into a dark tar-pot of loneliness and despair. As I saddled up the grey mare and prepared to leave the high plains of the central plateau, my thoughts fell on my own family. I stood still, as if in a dream, unmoving; these thoughts rounded me as once my father's dogs rounded so many of the island's tigers.

What have you done, Myko? I thought, what have you done?

The grey, keen to stretch her legs, splashed in the wet soil with her front hooves. I placed a calming hand on her withers where her coat ran smooth and ivory-coloured. For a moment she calmed, but then she roused again, straining at her bit and cleaving the air with white breath from her flared nostrils. I could not constrain her for long; as I dug my heel in her broad flank she quickly broke free.

The grey's stride gathered up pace as we ploughed, robust and restless, through the dark tree-bordered scrub. Her legs strained ready to the task for some time, but my own limbs trembled as I sat tightly on her back, ducking the sweep of ropey wet branches.

A slow wind breezed among the reed-sheaves and the steady rainfall washed the sloughed bark strips in the grey's path, but failed to slow her. For miles she galloped on, beating hard through the forests and lower foothills until we reached the silver fields of bracken on the edge of the plains.

The expanse of air calmed the grey's ardour and she dropped into a settled trot. I felt relieved to give up the wild galloping, but as we travelled slowly towards the sparse vegetation of the gulch that skirted the central plateau, I found my own emotions begin to alter.

Thoughts of my father's face on the night I deserted my family stampeded on my mind. I had not believed he held any feelings before then, but now I saw the blood leave his cheeks again and I followed his eyes as they pitched from side to side, searching for the answer to my accusations. I tried to push away the idea, but it did not subside.

The rain stopped falling as I looked up from the grey's back. The sky above was lit with a wide flash of amethyst. At its edges the deep blue turned to black and then the sun slid beneath the horizon. A moon was already waiting to take the sun's place and the air felt still and cool. Night approached fast. On the island, all was as it should be.

About the Author

Tony Black was born in NSW, Australia and grew up in Scotland and Ireland. An award-winning writer, The Last Tiger is his 12th novel. He lives in Scotland with his wife and son.

tonyblack.net